Little
Sam Mountain

Charles C. Fletcher

2010
Parkway Publishers, Inc.
Boone, North Carolina

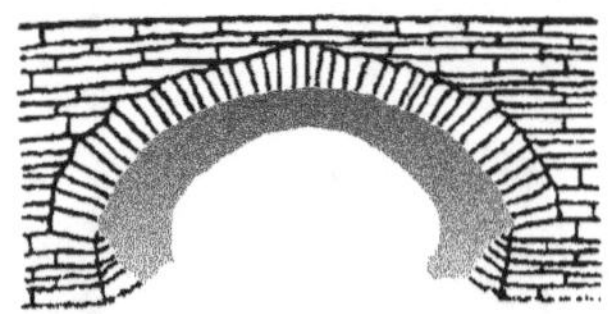

Published by
Parkway Publishers, Inc.
PO Box 3678
Boone, North Carolina 28607
Ph. & Fax: (828) 265-3993
www.parkwaypublishers.com

Contents

Foreword

The story of John Dowdy, a young boy that never knew anything about the rest of the world until he left his home on "Little Sam Mountain" is typical of those that lived in the mountains of Western North Carolina, Virginia, New York State and other remote areas of the United States. This was their way of escaping the hard life that their parents, Grandparents and their ancestors had before them.

The older generation understands this story and it will give the younger reader some idea of what life was like in the "backwoods" of America during and after the years of the Great Depression.

Charles C. Fletcher

Home On Little Sam

John Dowdy had never dreamed that someday he would leave the ridge on Little Sam Mountain near the watershed that supplied the water for the town of Canton. "The shed", as it was called, was located on the Beaverdam side of Little Sam Mountain. John and his family lived near the fence that was around the watershed.

This was the place in the mountains of western North Carolina where John was born and where he had lived the seventeen years of his life. A new world was about to open up for John. He had never given any thought to leaving the mountain and his family.

It was 1939 and the world was beginning to recover from the Great Depression of the early 30s. Old industries were starting to operate again and new ones were being built. There was a war going on in Europe and there was a great demand for almost anything that was for sale.

It was early fall -- the season of the year that John liked best. All the crops were laid by, and there was very little work going on at the top of Little Sam.

"Dad," John said, "would it be all right with you if I took off early tomorrow morning and go to town? I was over at the Smiths the other day and the oldest boy, Sam, was in town last week. He said that nearly everyone was really excited. Said they were talking about a big war in the countries across the ocean. Some country is trying to take all the other countries and make them a part of theirs. The government is asking for men to join the Army. I want to find out what he was talking about. I could hang around the blacksmith shop and the benches under the trees on Main Street." This was where all the latest happenings were talked about. "I'll be back before dark tomorrow."

His Dad scratched his head, waited a few minutes, then said, "Better get to bed early so you can get up in time to feed the cow and horse before you go. Don't need to start before it gets a little daylight. Could miss the trail in the dark and fall off a rock cliff. Some mighty high ones on Little Sam. Better wear your shoes -- pretty rocky when you get to the Crabtree Road. Probably take about three hours to make the trip. Oh. Better take one of the older hens and sell her at the store. You'll need something to eat at dinnertime. The store man will probably give you fifty cents if she is good and fat. If you have any money left, bring it back and give it to your mama. She saves to buy cloth for the girls' clothes."

John went up the ladder to the loft of the log house. This was where he and his younger brother slept. He didn't waste any time getting in bed, but he couldn't go to sleep. He was thinking of all the places he would visit in town. He'd go to the drug store, hardware, café, livery stable, blacksmith shop and all the other places to get the latest news so he could tell the others at home when he got back the next evening.

A Trip To Town

John was out of bed and dressed a long time before daylight. He went to the barn and fed the cow and horse. His next stop was the chicken house. He ran his hands over the chickens looking for a big fat one. He finally chose one, took it to the house, found some string, and tied its legs together. He didn't want her to get loose on the way to town. He would need the money from selling this hen if he was to eat anything today.

Everything was ready, and he was on his way to the city. It was beginning to show some sign of daylight -- enough for John to follow the trail off the mountain to where it ended at the Crabtree Road. This was a narrow dirt road that crossed the mountain between Thickety on the east side of the two mountains to the community of Crabtree on the west side. There was very little travel along this road. Every now and then, someone on horseback or riding a wagon would go by. This road was a sort of a short cut to Canton.

By the time he was off the mountain, it was full daylight and the families that lived along the road were out doing their morning work around their farms. They would wave at John and sometimes would holler, "Howdy". Of course, John didn't know any of these people. He had only been off the mountain a few times with his dad.

At the next farm John passed, the man who lived there was at his mailbox on the side of the road. He said, "Good morning. What are you doing out so early? Where did you get that chicken? Didn't steal it, did you?"

It was a few moments before John said anything. He let this stranger get through asking his questions.

"I brought this hen from home," he said. "Going to sell her to some city folks in town. I hear that they can't keep chickens, hogs, or any animals in town. Someone will want this chicken. Make a big pot of chicken and dumplings for someone."

"How 'bout selling her to me? I don't want to eat her. Need a good laying hen, and she sure looks like a good 'n. How much for her?" he asked.

"I think she'll bring a dollar."

"Now that's a little steep, don't you think?"

"That's the price," John said.

The man took a leather pouch from his overall pocket, snapped it open, took a good look inside, and said, "I only got seventy-five cents. Will you sell her for that?"

"Don't know. Let me think about it for a minute."

"Well...," John said. "I hate to think about someone killing this pretty hen, and it's a long way to town yet, and my arm's getting a little tired. Give me the seventy-five cents, and you can have her. I'll be losing money, but it's best for both of us. You get a good egg laying hen, and I'm keeping her from being killed and put in a pot with a bunch of dumplings."

The sale was made, and John was on his way again. As he walked on toward town, he had a smile on his face. The way he saw it, he had made an extra twenty-five cents on selling that chicken. The man at the store would never give over fifty cents and sometimes less.

Now John had never been to a public school. He and the other children in his family were taught how to read and write by their mother. Their mom had finished the sixth grade in a school up the river toward Mount Pisgah. She had kept all her books, and when she married and moved to the log house on Little Sam, she brought them with her. It seemed that the women folks were believers in an education, but the men folks weren't. The men said all they needed to know was how to work. The teaching from John's mom was beginning to pay dividends. The sale of the hen was the first of many deals that he would make in his life.

Uncle Tom's Mill

John was soon at the General Store and water-powered grist mill. This was where the streets were paved and the city began. His first stop would be at the grist mill, which was operated by an old man with a long white beard. Everyone called him "Uncle Tom". He was up to date on all the latest news.

Uncle Tom's grist mill was where everyone in this end of Haywood county brought their corn to be ground into meal. The water wheel was very slow, and Uncle Tom was a good match for the water wheel. He never seemed to be in any hurry. The two of them were made for each other. No one knew where he came from. He just happened to be there on the day that the owner of the mill needed someone to run the mill. He had operated a mill somewhere else but, that place was never revealed to anyone. All in all, Uncle Tom did a good job and, most of all, everyone enjoyed being around him.

The door was always open when the mill was running, and Uncle Tom was always sitting on a nail keg by the meal hopper. There was a wide crack in the floor near where he sat, and he would spit tobacco juice through it and watch to see it hit the pool of water under the mill.

Uncle Tom looked up as John entered and said, "Hi young feller. Ain't seen you in nearly a year. How you been? Been busy up on the mountain?"

"I come down to get some news on the war that I heard about. The oldest boy at the Smiths, who live a few miles from me, was telling me that there was talk of a war."

Uncle Tom spat out a cud of tobacco and began to tell Tom what he had heard about the war.

"Well, it seems that there is a country over the waters that has a president who wants to take over all other countries so he can run 'em. They say that this feller was a painter and he joined the Army and become a corporal. Then he got a gang of his buddies together and started taking over little places at first and then got him a bigger Army and started takin' over whole countries."

"Uncle Tom, I hear that our Army is signing up most anyone who'll join. You were in the World War. What was it like?"

Uncle Tom hadn't talked about his service during the First World War but a few times. When he did say anything about it, it was always about the good parts. He never talked about shooting and things like that.

"Well, the Army gives you some money, plenty of good food, and good warm clothing. If you get sick they have good doctors to take care of you so you'll be well again. It's not too bad."

Then he stopped, took out a plug of "Red Coon" tobacco, and cut himself a big chew. I knew that it would be a waste of words to ask him anything else about his war.

"Got to be going," John said. "Lots of things to do in town before I head back home to Little Sam. See you next time I come to town."

"Good luck", said Uncle Tom.

A Day In Town

When John reached the center of town he didn't see many people . This was a Tuesday, and only the people who had business to take care of came to town during the regular weekdays. Saturday was the big day for people to come to town. Nearly everyone for miles around would be there on a Saturday. This was their day off from work and a day for visiting.

John did find a lot of the older men at the blacksmith shop and on the benches under the trees on Main Street. They were trading knifes and talking about the war. One of the men, who was sixty or more years old, was talking: "If any of them furiners come over here and try to take my farm, I'll tell you right now, he'll have a fight on his hands. I can still shoot a squirrel's eye out at a hundred yards."

Another man spoke up. "Mr. Pless who owns the hardware store over near the bridge says that he is selling all the guns he can get. And everyone is wanting cartridges for their guns. Sure hope that all they will need them for is to shoot crows and hawks. I would hate to shoot a man for no reason."

The day had passed quickly for John. He had a good day. He had eaten two ten-cent hotdogs and drunk a couple of "Nehi" soft drinks. And, he had money left from the sale of the hen to give to his for Mom to buy cloth with.

Charles C. Fletcher

Big Plans For The Future

It was nearly dark when John arrived back at the log house. Everyone was waiting for him with a thousand questions about his trip. He was tired, but he answered some of their questions with a promise to tell them everything tomorrow. He soon went up the ladder to the loft of the house where his brother and he slept. He was tired. It had been a big day for John.

The next day was routine: feeding the animals, cutting wood, and doing other small chores around the house. There were a lot of questions from his brother and two younger sisters. But it was agreed that John would tell about his trip to town that night after they had eaten supper. This didn't keep the girls from asking about what he did in town.

"If you girls will quit following me around, I'll tell you what I ate for dinner yesterday."

"We promise," they said.

"Well, you remember that I took one of the hens and sold her for seventy five cents. Have you seen the café next to the feed and hardware store down at the end of town? The one nearly at the river bridge? They sell only sandwiches to eat, including hotdogs, and "dopes" (soda pop) to drink. They also have a shooting gallery around back where several men were shooting at targets. Don't know what kind of game they were playing. I ordered me two hotdogs and one of those big Nehi orange drinks. The hotdogs had a load of chili and onions on them. The tomato catsup was free, and I really poured it on them dogs. This was about the best eating I ever had. And the whole bill was only twenty five cents -- a dime each for the dogs and a nickel each for the big oranges. I would have brought you girls one but it would have been cold and not tasted very good by the time I got back."

"We could have warmed them on the stove," one of them said. "We never saw a hotdog. Dad never takes us along when he goes to the store. Promise that the next time you go you'll bring us one. And a big orange drink. We've never tasted one of them either."

"I'll think on it," John said.

When everyone had eaten supper, the dishes were put away, and everyone was gathered in the "sitting room", John told all about his trip to the city.

"Sure is a big place and nearly everybody is in a hurry. Don't know where they are going. Lots of talk about the war and how our government wants all the men they can get to join the Army."

Soon everyone was yawning and ready to go to bed. Tomorrow would be another ordinary day for the Dowdy family.

After dinner the next day John, his brother, and his father were sitting under a big shade tree near the house.

"Dad," John said, "what do you think about me joining the

Army? I heard in town the other day that about all the boys are joining. They said that you have to be eighteen years old, but if you are big for your age you can join anyhow. Hardly anyone has a birth certificate. The Army soldier who comes to Canton every Monday don't ask too many questions.

"John, you're only seventeen years old. Do you think you could make a good soldier as young as you are?"

"Well, Dad, I am pretty big for my age and as stout as a mule from all the hard work I've done working in the fields ever since I was six or seven. After all, I'll be leaving the mountain and the family one of these days pretty soon. Got to make it on my own. Maybe find me a wife some day. The only the girls who I know are my sisters and the Smith girls. I shore don't want one of them Smiths."

After a few minutes his dad said, "I guess you are thinking like a man; so, if you want to try for the job and be a soldier, you have my blessing. Can't expect you to stay here forever. You should talk it over with your mom, though. I know that the thought of losing one of her children will cause her to break down and cry. Women cry real easy."

"I know. I'll talk with her when she gets all of her morning work done and is sitting down to rest a bit. Hope she doesn't cry. She seems so happy all the time. I don't know how in the world she gets all her work done -- washing clothes, cooking three meals every day, and all the little things she does for us children. Mom sure is one of a kind. Dad, you sure are lucky to have found you a wife like Mom. Sure hope I do as well when I choose me a wife."

John had made his mind up and had the blessings from his family. The next thing for him was to make another trip to town and talk with the recruiting soldier about signing up. He planned to go next Monday. He'd get up real early and leave as soon as it was light enough to see. He told his dad about his plans and went on his way the following Monday.

Signing Up

It didn't take him as long to get to town this time because he didn't stop at the corn mill, and he didn't take a hen to sell. He planned to get done with the signing up for the Army and be back home in time for supper that night.

John found the recruiting soldier at the Trailway bus station and started talking with him.

"My name is John Dowdy. There is talk around that you want to sign up as many men as you can to be soldiers in the US Army.

The recruiter took a big sip of the coffee he was drinking and asked, "How old are you?"

"Eighteen," John said.

"You look big enough. Have you got your birth certificate? Don't look like you've started shaving yet."

"None of my family or any of the people on Little Sam have certificates. The only record of our birthday is wrote in the family Bible. Granny Jones who lives with the Smith family is what everybody calls 'midwife'. When it's time for a new baby to be born, somebody gets word to Granny and tells her where it will be. She has a little black leather bag that she takes along. Don't know what's in the bag. Anyhow, she helps the women give birth."

"Let me tell you a few things that you should know before you sign up. After signing the enlistment papers you will get to go back home for a week. You will report back to this bus station the next Monday morning at eight o'clock to go for a physical examination. We don' want sick soldiers. If you pass your physical you will come back here and have one more week at home before going somewhere for your basic training.

"Once you have signed the papers there is no backing out. All of the clothing you will need will be given to you. You will be paid twenty-one dollars every month. There are other things that your sergeant or commanding officer will tell you later on. Do you still want to join our Army?"

"I sure do," John said. "Twenty-one dollars is a lot of money. Ain't never had that much money."

"OK," said the recruiter. See you on Monday morning at eight o'clock. Want to go up the street to the Greek café and have lunch?"

"I reckon not. I didn't bring any money with me. I plan to get back home by suppertime."

"Come on. This will be your first meal on Uncle Sam. I'll pay and get my money back from the paymaster back at camp."

When we got to the café, the recruiter ordered a big meal and said, "Tell the young lady what you want."

"Have you got any hotdogs?" John said.

"We sure do," she said. "Want everything on them?"

"What's everything?"

"Homemade chili, onions, Cole slaw, and a big fat wiener. How many do you want?"

"Two will be enough. Have you got a Nehi orange," he asked?

"Sure," she said.

"I'll have one of them, too. Oh, and bring some tomato ketchup."

"Coming right up. Only be a minute."

John sure was hooked on hotdogs and orange dopes.

"I ate a couple of these the last time I was in town," John told the recruiter. "Have you ever eaten at the café and shooting gallery at the other end of town? They sure make good hotdogs. I don't think they have anything else to eat. At least, I didn't see anybody eating anything but hot dogs."

John drowned the dogs with ketchup, and they were gone before his new-found friend had eaten the garden salad that was a part of his dinner.

"I'd better get started back home," John said. "The days are getting shorter, and it gets dark earlier than it did during the summer. I sure thank you for the dinner. I'll buy your dinner when I get that twenty-one dollars."

John wiped ketchup from his mouth with the napkin that the waiter brought along with the dogs and said, "See you Monday."

On his way back up Little Sam, a million thoughts were running through John's mind. When he was within sight of the log house he could see his brother and sisters standing outside looking down the trail watching for him.

When they saw John coming up the path they all came running to meet him. When they were close they began asking all kinds of questions.

"Whoa," John said. "Wait till I get to the house and catch my breath, and I'll tell you all about what happened today."

They quieted down a bit, and the girls walked along holding their big brother's hand. Like the children in all the families of these mountains, they loved each other. Although they were poor in worldly things, they were one big happy family.

John spent a lot of time with his mom telling her all the things she could do with the money he would be sending home.

"Twenty-one dollars is a lot of money," John said. "Dad will have to got to town at least once every week to pick up the mail. I'll be writing a lot so you will know what I am doing and where I'm at. I'll send money when I get paid at the end of each month. I won't need much for myself because they are giving me my clothes, all my meals, and anything else I need. Yes m'am, I think that this will be great. There'll be no more plowing ,cutting wood, or sleeping in that cold loft in the winter time."

The week went really slow for John. He thought about all the things that might happen in the following weeks, months, and years.

"Wait a minute," he thought. "I can't get to town before eight o'clock on Monday if I have to wait for daylight before leaving. I don't know anyone who I could spend the night with on Sunday. I've got to think of some way to be there on time. If I'm not, they'll leave without me. I know what I'll do. To-morrow morning I'll go down to the corn mill and ask Uncle Tom if I can spend Sunday night at the mill. I don't think that he locks it up, anyway. I could use some of the 'tow sacks' for a bed. It would only take me about twenty minutes to get to the bus station from the mill. Yessir, that's what I'll do."

The Bus Ride

John spent Sunday night in the mill, but he didn't sleep much. It seemed he took only a few catnaps. He was thinking about being on time and what would he would be doing tomorrow.

When he arrived at the bus station, there were only two other boys there. They were sitting at a counter drinking coffee.

"That Army bus hasn't gone, has it? he asked one of the boys.

"No," one of them said. "It'll be another thirty or forty minutes before it gets here. We live here in town and came a little early so we would have time to eat some breakfast."

"You had breakfast yet," the other boy asked.

"I'm not hungry. Sort of lost my appetite. Guess I'm a little nervous, signing up for the Army and everything."

"You going in the Army? We're signed up, too," one of them said. Don't know where we're going. Heard someone say that it's to an Army camp in South Carolina. Hear that they'll pick up some boys in Waynesville then come by here. Won't be long now. Better have a cup of coffee. They don't charge the boys who're going into the Army."

"In that case, I might as well," John said.

The bus was a few minutes late, and there were about ten people waiting to get on. There was seven or more already on the bus. The bus loaded up and headed toward Asheville on Highway 19-23.

It was pretty quiet on the bus. There were only a few whispers between some who knew each other. One was telling the fellow sitting beside him that he heard the bus driver say that he had to pick up some recruits in Asheville.

Time went by really fast, and it seemed like only a few minutes until the bus was pulling into the station in Asheville. There were a bunch of boys waiting to get on board. When all of them were seated, the bus was completely full.

The bus pulled out onto the main road and was off to some place that John had never been. The only place he had ever been besides the top of Little Sam was the town of Canton.

The bus was soon out of the mountains of western North Carolina and in a country that was nearly level. There were lots of fields of small trees. John heard someone say they were peach orchards. The farther they went, the leveler it was, and clay soil had turned to sand. John's eyes were wide open. He had never dreamed that there were places like this in this world.

After about three hours, the bus pulled off the road and headed toward a field filled with row upon row of wooden buildings. There was a high fence around the whole field where the buildings were. The bus stopped at a gate where two soldiers were standing. They had bands around their arms with the letters "MP" on them. The bus driver opened the door and said something to one of them. He motioned for us to go on in.

The Physical

The bus pulled up along side of another bus. John noticed that there were several buses there. He was greeted by an Army sergeant when he got off the bus.

"Make two lines and follow me," said the sergeant.

John was led into one of the buildings and was met by other soldiers. He was taken into a room and seated at a table. The soldiers gave everyone a pack of papers.

"You are going to take a little test. Can you all read?" asked one of the soldiers."

Everyone raised his hand except one. This was a boy who was on the bus when it came to pick John up.

"You can't read mister?"

"Not very good. Just a little. I'll do the best I can. Sure want to join this Army."

"OK," said the soldier. "Do your best."

Most all the questions on the test didn't make sense. There were things like "if you push the handle on the back of a boat to the right, which way will the boat go?" John had never seen a boat. There wasn't any need for one on Little Sam Mountain. But John put some kind of an answer beside all the questions on the test.

The testing soldier hollered out, "Time is up. Hand in your papers and go to the building next to this one. Some one will show you where to go."

One of the boys from Asheville said, "That was our IQ test." Pretty hard, too."

"Don't know what they are looking for. Don't need to know which way a boat would go. The Army don't have boats. It's the Navy has boats," John said.

"Everybody fall in behind the sergeant. It's lunchtime. He will take you to the mess hall, and after you eat he will take you to the exam building to find out if you are ready for the Army."

John and all the other men were taken into a long building with row upon row of tables with benches on both sides. On one side of the room there was a long table-like counter where the food was. Behind this there were about eight or ten men wearing white aprons.

"You men get a tray, a plate, and a small bowl. Also get a knife, fork, and a spoon. Go down the line and tell the KP what you want to eat."

John was near the front of the line. As he got closer, his eyes bulged out. He had never seen so much food or had he ever seen so many different kinds of food. He started down the line and was taking a little bit of everything. About half way through the line he stopped and asked one of the KPs, "Do you have any hotdogs?"

The KP was dumbfounded. He gave John a good look, sort of smiled and said. "No, we don't have any hotdogs today. We usually have them on a Saturday or Sunday."

"I sure wish today was Saturday. I really like hotdogs, especially with a lot of tomato ketchup on them."

After they had finished their lunch, the sergeant took them into a big room in a building near the mess hall. As they entered each one was given an oblong basket.

"Take off all your clothes, put them in the basket, and form a line behind me."

"I don't like to run around with all my clothes off," John said. "I'll get cold and, besides that, I don't like for people to see me naked."

"Do as you are told," said a sergeant. Ain't no one going to bother you. Now, get with it."

John still didn't like the idea of showing off what Mother Nature had given him, but off came his clothes. He had never dreamed that he would ever see what he saw in that room, and he hoped he would never see it again. All the country boys were ashamed. The city boys didn't seem to mind. Maybe they had done this before.

All the men with the white coats were doctors. They were going to see if the recruits were healthy enough to be soldiers. The line started moving. Down the line doctor after doctor would check different things. One the eyes ,another the ears, the hands, legs, feet, teeth, tongue, and all the other parts of the body. The last two doctors in the line had big, long needles. One took the right arm and the other the left.

"Won't hurt a bit," one of them said.

"Wham," in went a needle, one on the left and one on the right.

"All done. Get your clothes back on."

They didn't have to tell John a second time. He was tired of everyone looking at him in his birthday suit. He had tried to hide some parts of his body with his hands.

When everyone had his clothes back on, they were taken into the next room. There they were greeted by a Captain who was wearing a pretty uniform with row on row of medals pinned to both sides of his coat.

"My name is Captain Pugh. I will finish the job of making you a soldier of the United States Army. I will give you the oath and swear you in. Everyone raise his right hand and repeat after me."

Up went the hands. A couple of the boys raised their left hands.

"Get that right hand up," the captain said.

He read the oath, and everyone repeated it after him. When he was finished everyone said, "I do."

"Well, men," the Captain said. "You are now soldiers with the rank of private in the United States Army." From this day on you will be told what to do and what not to do. You don't have to think, we will do all the thinking for you. Sergeant, give them their first orders."

Each one was given an envelope of papers.

"You will be taken back to your hometowns. You have exactly one week to get all your business in order. You will then report to the recruiting officer who signed you up. He will give you your orders. Does every one understand?"

No one spoke up. They were all tired from all that had happened to them since eight o'clock that morning. John and the others were glad to be back on the bus and on their way back home.

Back Home

When the bus arrived at the station in Canton, it was almost dark. John knew that there was not enough time before complete darkness for him to get home. The only thing to do was stay at the mill another night and go home early the next morning. Uncle Tom had told John that he could sleep in the mill building any time he wanted to. He would have to do without supper, but this was no problem. He had eaten so much at the mess hall for dinner he wasn't hungry at all.

"Hope the family doesn't worry about me," John said to himself. I'll get up early and be home before dinner."

When he arrived home the next morning around ten o'clock, his Mom, the girls, and his brother saw John at a distance. They began to wave their hands to him. As he got closer the girls ran to meet him.

The questions were fast and many from the girls and his brother. Mom didn't have a chance to ask him about what went on at the Army camp.

"When I catch my breath and we have eaten dinner, we all

will sit out under the big shade tree, and I will tell you what went on with me at the Army camp."

All of the family gathered together in the shade of the big maple tree out in the yard.

"Are you all ready to hear about my trip yesterday?"

The girls began to clap their hands and hollow. "Go ahead, John. Don't leave out anything."

"Well ...," John began. "I slept a couple of nights in the corn mill building. The bus ride was OK. I saw a lot of things I had never seen. Some of the towns we went through were big with real high buildings."

He continued with his account of the trip. After answering many questions, he paused, looked at each member of the family, cleared his throat, and said, "When I leave next Sunday, I won't be able to come see you all for at least three months. This is the time that they say it takes to train before we become real soldiers. One of the boys on the bus was saying that a friend of his who was a soldier and had finished this training told him that it was pretty tough. Said there was an Army officer with you everywhere you went and was always telling you what to do. The country boys made it pretty good, but the ones from the big cities were not used to hard work, and they had to try a lot harder to keep up with the training. I don't want you to worry about me; and when I can come home, I will be wearing my uniform. I'll make you all proud of your big brother.

As John looked at his family, he noticed tears in their eyes. "Well," he said. "Let's all go back to the house. Mom has made a pot of coffee, so we will celebrate my joining the Army. The week will be gone before we know it.

John visited all the animals as though they were his brothers and sisters. He had a good talk with old Nellie, the horse. "I know you will miss me hollowing at you all the time when you are plowing," John said.

Old Nellie looked at John with her big blue eyes, wiggled her lips and made a funny noise as if she were saying, "I'll miss you too, John."

The old hound dogs were at John's heels all that week. John and the dogs had spent a lot of time together over the past years. They hunted all kinds of animals to supply food for the family. Even the other creatures around the house seemed to know that there was going to be a change in the family.

The Party

On Friday evening, the Smith family, who lived on the next ridge, came to visit with John and his family. A little later, here came the Robinson clan, the mother, the father, and a bunch of girls and boys of different ages. Must have been ten of them. We didn't know this family very well because they lived at the foot of the mountain on the Crabtree side. Dad knew them pretty well from trading cows & hogs with them and from other dealings he had with them.

The yard and house were soon full of people. Some had brought their musical instruments along with them: a fiddle, banjo, a guitar, and even a washboard. Something was about to happen that John didn't know about. His dad went into the house and returned with his banjo.

"All right everybody," Dad said. "Find you a partner and get ready for a good old fashioned dance. We're going to celebrate my oldest son, John, who's leaving tomorrow to serve in the United States Army. He is going to help get rid of that feller that's causing all the trouble across the ocean. What tune do you want to hear?"

No one spoke up.

"How about 'Sourwood Mountain'? We'll do 'Barbra Allen' and some of the others later."

The music started and, the younger ones had chosen partners and were dancing all over the yard. Soon everyone had joined in except John and the oldest Smith girl. Her name was Sarah. The times when John had visited the Smiths, he had never paid any attention to Sarah. She was about sixteen years old. She had curled her hair and wore her Sunday dress. John couldn't take his eyes off her. She was looking at John every now and then. When she thought John was looking at her she would smile.

After a while, John moseyed over to where Sarah was standing and said, "I'm John. I'll be leaving in the morning. Do you dance?" he asked.

"Not too good," she said. "But I'll try if you want to dance with me."

"OK, let's give it a try," John said.

As they danced John said, "You know what? I've been over to your house to visit your big brother, Sam, but I don't think I ever saw you."

"You saw me, but never remembered. I saw you every time you came over, but kept to myself. Didn't think you would care to talk with me."

John didn't say anything for a few seconds and then said, "Sarah, I think you are the prettiest girl I've ever seen. That is, besides my mom. I'll be gone for a spell while I'm in the Army. Would you like for me to write you a letter every now and then? I would like for you to write to me. You could tell me what's going on here on the mountain. I'll tell you about the Army if you want to hear about it."

"John, I think I like you a lot. I'll write to you if you'll answer my letters."

"That's a deal, John said. "Probably won't have time to write for the first three months. Everyone I have talked with said that the Army kept you busy night and day. But I will write. I'll send my letters to the post office in Canton. Some of your family go to town every now and then."

"That will be fine. I can walk to town and get the mail. It's not more than six or seven miles."

Sarah and John spent the rest of the evening talking more than dancing. It was getting late, nearly ten o'clock. Everyone began getting their families together, saying good bye, and heading for home.

"Sarah," John said. "Would you care if I walked you home?"

"No," Sarah said. "I was hoping that you would ask."

John went into the house and came back with a kerosene lantern.

"Better take this along. Could fall off a rock cliff if we got off the trail."

Sarah sort of laughed.

Off they went toward the Smith's house, holding hands and talking about their future letters and the fun they had that night. It was the beginning of a love affair between two young people who lived on Little Sam Mountain.

Off To Camp

It was Sunday morning, and everyone in the Dowdy family were awake and out of bed a long time before they usually woke up. This was an important day for them. This was the day when their oldest son was leaving for the Army. After breakfast the same questions were asked that were asked every day this past week: Where will you be stationed? Who is going with you from Canton who you know? Are you going on the bus or the train? John couldn't answer their questions. He didn't know any of the answers.

"I ironed your good shirt and overalls," Mom said to John. "I read in the papers you brought back from the camp in South Carolina that you didn't need to bring any extra clothes. It said that you would be issued everything that you would need when you arrived at your camp. Better leave after dinner so you can make you a place to sleep at the corn mill. Sure is nice of Uncle Tom to let you stay there. "Here is a dollar. You may need something to eat before you get to camp. Don't' want my boy to go hungry and get skinny. I hear that the Army likes big healthy soldiers. I bet you will be one of the best," she said to John.

Dinner was soon on the table. Today there was something special. Mom had killed one of the chickens and made a big pot of chicken and dumplings. The only time they had chicken was at Christmas and Thanksgiving. John's mother said today was as important as either of those holidays -- maybe more important. When John left, they never knew when they would see him again.

When dinner was over, John hugged his mom and the girls. He shook his dad's hand, and he put his hand on his brother's shoulder and said, "You help Dad. Eat and grow fast, and in another year or so you can join the Army, and maybe we can be stationed at the same camp.

John felt a lump coming up in his throat, so he knew it was time to say, "good bye," and head toward town and the corn mill.

"See you all soon," he said. Then he turned and went down the trail toward the road to Crabtree. He didn't look back.

When he arrived at the bus station the next morning, the same boys who he went with for the physical were there. John spoke to them but didn't join in their conversation. He wasn't a talker. He said he could learn more by listening.

The bus was on time and, like the other time, there were several already on the bus when it stopped for John and the others at Canton. After they were all on the bus, the soldier who had signed them up got on the bus.

"Let me have your attention," he said. "I am putting Frank Hill in charge of this trip. You will stay with him and do what he says for you to do. Do you all understand? I went over everything about this trip with him yesterday. He has the orders in this folder. Good luck." Then he got off the bus, and he shut the bus door.

The bus was on the road toward Asheville, but this didn't give John any hint as to where they were going. "I'll ask the bus driver," John said.

"Well, I can tell you that we'll stop in Charlotte for lunch. That's all I can tell you," said the driver.

John went back to his seat. "Wouldn't help any if we knew where we were going," he thought. "May get some idea where we are going after we leave Charlotte. There're not many Army camps in North Carolina."

Everyone was looking out the windows. To most of them, they were in strange surroundings. Most were like John. They had never been more than a few miles from their homes around the mountains of Western North Carolina.

"Shore is a big world," someone said. "Seems like the hills are going away. Getting kind of level out there."

John closed his eyes and kind of dozed off. He didn't sleep very well at the corn mill last night. A million thoughts went through his mind, but he finally fell asleep. It was only about five minutes until John was wide awake. Rubbing his eyes, it occurred to him that he hadn't spoken to the fellow sitting beside him on the bus.

"My name is John Dowdy," he said. "What is your name?"
"Bill Wolf," he said.
"You were on the bus when it came to Canton where I got on. Where do you live?"
"Over near the Indian Reservation at Cherokee. In a little village called Maggie Valley. The Indian land starts after you cross the top of Soco Mountain. I may be a little kin to the Cherokee tribe. Mama looks like an Indian. Long black hair and high cheeks. Where you from?" Bill said.
"I live on the top of Little Sam Mountain. It's near Canton. That's where I got on the bus. Our house is about five or six miles

from town. We never go to Canton unless we need something from the store. We grow about everything that we need.

"They tell me that in the Army most everyone has a special buddy. Someone he can trust and go to when he needs a little help. What do you say about you and me becoming Army buddies while we are taking our training? We may be lucky enough to go to the same location after we finish."

"OK with me," Bill said. "I was thinking about this before you asked me. We'll take care of each other the best we can."

The scenery was changing very fast along the road as we were getting closer to Charlotte. Cotton fields all along both sides of the road.

John said, "Bill, look at that dirt. Don't look like the black dirt back home. Looks more like sand than dirt. Couldn't grow corn in a place like this. Seeing a lot of cotton mills near every little town we come to. I hear that lots of people work in them. Don' think the owner of the mill pays the workers much. Just enough for them to get by on.

"Bill, look way over there. See them tall buildings? Bet we are getting close to Charlotte. Sure hope so. I ain't had anything to eat since I left home on Sunday. Sure would like a couple of hotdogs and a big orange drink. Have you ever eaten a hotdog with lots of chili and onions on it?"

Bill said, "Don't recall ever eating one. In fact, I never heard of one. Where we live is sort of like where you live. We also grow all of our food. Never been to Waynesville but a couple of times. Ain't never eaten in a café. We never had much money. We had to sell some chickens or a hog to get money to buy what we needed and couldn't grow at home on the farm."

The bus with its load of new soon-to-be soldiers pulled into the parking lot of a big building. This was where they were to eat lunch before going on to an Army camp that they didn't know the whereabouts of.

Frank Hill, the fellow who was appointed to be in charge of the trip went to the front of the bus. "All right, men," he said. "Follow me. This is where we are to eat lunch. All of you follow me to the cafeteria. You are not to go anywhere else. After you finish eating you are to come back to your same seat on the bus. Do you all understand? Straight back to the bus. All of you took the oath of a soldier, and if you don't do as I say you will be punished."

"He sure let the 'Being In Charge' go to his head," John said. "Must think he is a sergeant already. Better do as he says. He could cause us some trouble."

As Frank led the way and the others were following him, something happened that John couldn't figure out. As he got close to the front door, it opened all by itself. It didn't have any door knobs or any handles . Opened like something magic. Bill and John were near the back end of the line.

"Let the others go on," John said to Bill.

Bill and John stayed back until all of the others were inside. Then that "Magic Door" did it again. It closed all by itself. John had a good look all around the door to see if there was someone pushing it open and closing it. The whole front of the building was glass and he couldn't see anyone who could be making that door work this way.

"Come on, Bill. We'd better get in and eat. They may run out of food."

They walked toward the door, and it opened again. "This place is haunted," John said.

They got a tray and started through the line where there were people to give you what food you wanted. The first thing John asked the food server was "Got any hotdogs?"

The waiter gave John a good hard look and then smiled and said, "Soldier, this is the best eating place in the whole city. We wouldn't stoop so low as to serve a hotdog. Move on."

John didn't really understand what the man said so he dropped the subject of his favorite food, the hotdog.

Soon they were back on the bus. Frank counted everyone to make sure that they were all on the bus. He said to the bus driver, "Everybody is on, so I guess we can go now."

It was not long until they were out of the big city and out in the country. There was a change in the crop that the farmers were growing. Every farm had one or more special buildings for curing tobacco before taking it to the auctions to be sold. A few farmers grew a little tobacco back in Western North Carolina. They hung it in a barn loft to air cure. The farmers out here had fires that made a lot of smoke to cure their tobacco.

John said to Bill, "These people live in houses that look a lot worse than the log house I live in. They're just shacks. Don't think it gets too cold here in the flat-lands. No snow like we have back home."

John and Bill were not missing a thing as they moved farther south. "My Mom said that there was another tribe of Indians in North Carolina besides the Cherokee tribe. She thinks that they are the Catawba tribe. They look like the Cherokee except their skin is a little darker. Must be the hot sunshine they have down here. I don't know much about Indians. Weren't any on Little Sam, and I never went to where they live in Cherokee."

The farther they went, the fewer houses and barns they saw. Plenty of pine trees and sand everywhere.

"Hope that place they are taking us looks better than these places," John said. "Wouldn't want to do a lot of marching in that sand. Bet there are a lot of snakes and lizards in them pine fields. Don't want nothing to do with any snake. I am afraid of them. I don't care if they are big or little. A snake is a snake; don't matter what size it be.

"I feel the same way," said Bill.

Fort Bragg

"We are getting close to a town," John said. "Look how close the houses are."

"What does that road sign say?" Bill said.

"'Welcome to Fayetteville,'" John said.

The bus went through town, and up the road a few miles there was another sign. This gave them the answer to what they all were asking: "Where are we going?" The sign read, "Fort Bragg Army Base -- Restricted Area".

"This is it," John said. "This is where they are going to make soldiers out of us poor mountain boys."

The bus had stopped at a gate where two soldiers stood with guns. On their arms were bands that read, "MP". The driver opened the door of the bus, and one of the soldiers got on the bus. The driver said, "Brought you another load of soldiers-to-be."

The MP said, "Been here before?"

"Several times," said the driver.

"Take them to the Welcome Center. I'll call and tell them that you are here."

The driver closed the door and drove inside the fenced in area. It seemed that all of Fort Bragg Army Base must have had a fence around it. They passed several buildings and stopped in front of a building that looked like the one they were at in South Carolina. In fact, all the buildings looked the same. When the bus stopped, an Army captain came out of the building and walked over to the bus.

Frank, the one who was in charge and had the orders in an envelope, got off the bus and handed the envelope to the captain.

"Thank you," he said to Frank. "All right, everyone. Off the bus and form two lines facing me."

"This is it," John whispered to Bill. "Our new home."

Army Introduction

The captain removed the papers from the envelope and said, "When I call your name, you say 'here' and move over to where Sergeant Brodsky is standing and form two lines."

He began calling names, and there were a lot of loud 'Here's'. Soon he said to the Sergeant, "All present and accounted for. They belong to you, Sergeant. You know where to take them. Carry on." With this the captain went back into the building near the guard gate.

"Welcome soldiers," the sergeant said. "I'll lead you to the supply room where you will be issued all of the clothes and equipment that you will need. But first we have a special treat and surprise for you. Follow me."

We passed a couple of buildings and entered one that had a sign that read, "Barber Shop".

"I think we are about to get a hair cut," said Bill.

"Looks that way," John replied. "I don't need one," John said. "Mom cut my hair right before I left home."

Inside the barber shop were six men standing behind chairs

the likes of which John had never seen.

"Welcome, men, to Fort Bragg's number one hair stylists' shop. If you gentlemen will have a seat, we will get started. Don't be bashful. Take any one of the chairs."

John took the second chair in the row. The barber said to John, "How would you like your hair cut?"

"I don't know much about hair cutting, so you fix it any way you want to."

The barber didn't know what to say. No one had ever given him an answer like John had. They usually told him how they wanted it cut.

"Well — uh --," he said. "I'll do the best I can."

The hair clippers were buzzing and the hair went flying. "Next customer," said the barbers.

As the soldiers went to the door at the other end of the building, their sergeant was having them stand in two lines. Everyone who came out of the barber shop had the same style of haircut: cut down to the skin, with all the hair gone. Sure was a funny looking sight. Some of the ones who had a big head of black curly hair now looked the same as the everyone else: completely bald.

"It'll grow back," John said to Bill. "You shore look funny though."

Didn't take long for the haircuts. "Follow me," said the sergeant.

"Wonder where we are going?" John said.

"Won't be another barber shop," said Bill. "None of us has any hair left."

The men walked past several buildings. They all looked the same.

"Here is your home," said the sergeant.

"D-7-3" was painted on a board nailed to the front of the building.

"Sergeant Davis is waiting inside to assign you to the bunk you will be using." He will be your leader and boss for the time you are here. Get in there and get a place . There are a lot of things to be done before bedtime."

Sergeant Davis was a pretty rough looking man. He was somewhere in his thirties, about six foot-two, close to two hundred pounds. His skin was tan from being outdoors most of the time.

He cleared his throat and said, "My name is Brad Davis. I am from a little town near Knoxville, Tennessee. You are the eighth bunch of rookies I have had in these barracks. You will call me 'Sergeant Davis' when speaking to me. The word 'Mister' is out. Do you understand? As long as you follow my orders and do as I say, we will get along just fine. Don't cross me up. If you do you will pay dearly for it. My job is to make a good soldier out of you, and I intend to do just that.

"We don't go by the time you are used to. The time here will be military time. An example is that what you would call 'seven AM' will be 'oh seven hundred hours'. Our time starts over after 2400. You will catch on soon.

"OK, find you a bunk. There are sheets and blankets and a pillow on each cot. Remember which one you chose and do not change your mind and try to take one that is already taken."

Bill and John were lucky. They went up the steps and chose the two bunks at the far end from where the stairs were. The Sergeant's room was at the other end.

"All right," said sergeant Davis. Fall out and line up in two rows. We will go to the mess hall and eat. When we are finished eating it's to the Supply Room."

Inside the mess hall dining room there were row on row of long tables. There were benches on each side. As the group went, in some of the men sat down.

"Get off it!" hollered the sergeant. "Everybody stand until we are all in. I'll give the order when to sit down."

"This is kind of like we do it at home," John said. Wonder if someone will say the blessing?"

Everyone had found a place, and they were told to take their seats. The men working in the mess hall began to bring big bowls and platters of food and set them on the tables. They were passed around, and everyone took what he wanted to eat. There was roast beef, mashed potatoes, green beans, and carrots along with hot bread rolls. John had never in his life time seen so much food. With all this food he looked all over for his favorite, a hotdog. Maybe they hadn't heard of them because he didn't see any.

The waiters who were serving the food would be called by their real names as soon as John found out that they were. For now they were called "KPs".

After everyone was stuffed, here came the desert -- big bowls of rice pudding. Most of these boys had never eaten any of this or ever heard of it.

"Everybody outside," the Sergeant said. "Follow me." We were off to the Supply Room.

"Line up and go to one of the supply clerks. They will issue you everything you will need while here at Fort Bragg."

John stepped up to where a supply clerk was waiting. The clerk asked, "What size shoes do you wear?"

"Don't know," John said. "Only got a pair of shoes every few years back home. Dad never said what size. Don't make much difference if they are not so tight to hurt your feet. I went barefooted all the time when it was warm enough."

The clerk was speechless. He had heard a lot of stories, but never one that he really believed until he heard what John said. "Let me see one of your feet," said the clerk.

John stuck out his foot.

"Better pull off one of the shoes. Can't tell how big your foot is with that big shoe on it."

John took off one of his shoes.

"Looks like about a size nine to me. How about your size of pants and shirt?"

Here again John didn't have any idea what the clerk was talking about. For John, clothes were something used to hide your nakedness and to keep you warm. He didn't know about sizes.

The clerk had to use his judgment and guess what size clothes John would need. He handed John a duffel bag and said, "As I hand you your supplies, you put them in the duffel bag and you can sort them out after you get back to the barracks. If you should get something that doesn't come close to being the right size for you, bring it back later and I will exchange it.

"Thank you, sir. Ain't never had so many clothes. Are you sure you have enough to spare? Don't want you to run out and some of the others not get anything. You gave me two of everything. One pair of pants and one shirt would be fine."

"NEXT!" said the clerk.

John went back to his barracks wondering what he would do with all these clothes. He returned to his bunk in the barracks and began to arrange his clothes in the foot locker at the foot of his bed. His sergeant had told everyone that 2100 was "lights out". This was the way the Army told you that it was bedtime. He also said that they would be instructed in the way their bunks were to be made. Something about "tucked corners" and "tight top".

"Lights out!" yelled Sergeant Davis. This was his way of telling everyone that it was nine o'clock (2100) and time for all new recruits to get to bed. He didn't have say it again. Everyone was tired from all that had happened today: the long bus ride, the hair cut, the new clothing, and a lot of other things in between.

It seemed to John that he had just gone to sleep when he suddenly was woken up. Some fool was outside blowing a horn, and all the lights came on in the barracks. This was the warning that it was 0600. In another thirty minutes they were to be dressed in their new clothes and out in front of the barracks for roll call.

"Better hurry," John said to his buddy, Bill. "Don't want to make that sergeant mad at us on our first roll call. Come on. He won't notice that our shoes are not laced up. It's pretty dark out there."

Down the stairs and out the door they went. This was only the beginning of the many mornings that John would be in the street at six thirty in the morning. Rain, snow, warm, or cold -- it made no difference. This army had a certain way of doing things, and nothing would change its schedule. Then back in the barracks for a few minutes.

"Mess call!" the sergeant hollored. Everyone out and into formation.

"What in the world is 'formation'?" John thought. He wasn't about to act dumb and ask. He went outside, and everyone was lining up in two lines.

"This must be formation," John was telling Bill when he heard the Sergeant say, "Right face!" "I guess he wants us to look toward our right," he whispered to Bill.

Some turned one way and others turned in the right direction. Sergeant Davis had one of the few smiles on his face that we would see while here at Fort Bragg. This man was all business.

"All right, let's all line up in the right direction. The Mess Hall is down the street to your right. You that don't want any breakfast can go back in the barracks. Let's go. Hut- hut- hut-. Doing great. Keep it up."

When John and the rest of the platoon had taken their places at the tables and were given the "Be seated" command, from their leader, they sat down. Then out came the KPs with big platters filled with scrambled eggs, sausage, hash brown potatoes, and big bowls of flour gravy. The bread for this morning was toast. John (and lots of the other boys) had never seen so much food for breakfast nor had they ever seen so many different kinds of food. The toast was a big treat for John. He had never had "store-bought" loaf bread. He always thought that only the rich city folks ate store-bought bread. Everyone else had home-made biscuits and corn bread. Along with all this food there was orange juice and coffee. Except for one time, the closest thing to real orange juice John had ever had was the "Nehi" that he had drunk with his hotdogs.

John took a big sip of orange juice, licked his lips, and said to Bill, who always was close to him, "You know something. I've only eaten a real orange once in my life time. Dad was at the store one time a few days before Christmas and Mr. Cagle, the man who owned the store gave Dad six oranges.

"Merry Christmas," he said. "Take these to your children. I don't recall you ever buying any oranges."

"No, sir," Dad said. "Never had any extra money. Hard to come by, you know."

John ate until he thought food was coming out of his ears. "Guess we may as well go back to the barracks and get ready for whatever the Sergeant wants us to do next," he said to Bill.

"Guess we might as well," Said Bill.

They headed out the door toward the barracks. "Never seen so much food in all my born days," John said.

"Me neither," Bill said. "Sure wish my by family could have been here. They shore would have liked to sit down to a table with all that food the KPs kept bringing out."

When everyone was back, the Sergeant called them all outside and said, "From this day on when we go anywhere we will go to-gether. We will be in formation, and we will march like soldiers are supposed to march. Fall out, and be back here in ten minutes."

The day held more surprises for the new soldiers. They each were issued a gas mask, a 30-30 rifle, a back-pack, and a half pup-tent. They were now fully equipped US Army soldiers.

The full platoon was outside sitting in a circle. Sergeant Davis was in the middle. "How many of you have fired a gun? he said.

About half of the hands went up. Before I'm through with you, there will not be a man in my platoon who doesn't know how to take this rifle apart and put it back together behind his back. There are two things that I expect you to have with you at all times while on duty: your rifle and your gas mask. There will be inspections without warning, and your gun had better be clean. Do you all understand what I said?"

"Better listen to what he is saying," John said to Bill. "He could make this army life pretty hard if you made him mad at you.

"I kind of like him," Bill said. I bet his job is as tough for him as he makes it for us. I'm going to do everything he asks me to do."

"Me, too", said John.

For the following three weeks John's platoon were given instructions on how to take care of their rifles, the way to put on their gas masks, how to march. It was pretty hard for the Sergeant and the two PFCs who were his helpers to get everyone in step with all the others, but at the end of the first month, they were all pros. Everyone knew every command that was given and executed it well. They were ready for their first parade before the Base General. Yes sir, they were now soldiers.

Rifle Range

Today was a big day for John. Sergeant Davis announced that the platoon were going to the rifle range. They would have real bullets and shoot at targets. All of the platoon loaded up in "6x6" trucks and headed to where they were to learn how to shoot an Army rifle.

John wouldn't have any problems with this. He had used a gun ever since he was five or six years old. He didn't hunt for sport; he helped to supply meat for the dinner table. He was taught to never kill more than the family needed.

After unloading from the trucks, everyone chose a partner. One of the two would pull the target while his buddy was shooting, and they would trade places when the other was done with his shooting.

John was first to shoot. His partner, Bill Wolf, would signal a perfect shot every time John fired. Sergeant Davis was watching and asked John where he learned to shoot.

"Heck, Sergeant Ain't no problem to hit that little circle in the center. It's sitting' there as still as a mouse. Back on Little

Sam I had to shoot squirrels and rabbits while they were running. Dad would get after me if I missed on the first shot. 'Can't waste bullets like that,' he would say. Cost too much to waste."

Sergeant Davis decided to see for himself if John was really hitting the bulls-eye every time, so he went to the pit where Bill was pulling the target for John. Every time John shot the target the Sergeant would place a piece of tape over the hole.

"BANG!" another hole in the center. Sergeant Davis couldn't believe what he was seeing. He returned to where John was at his firing station and said, "Private Dowdy," I want you to help me show these rookies how to shoot a gun. You don't need any practice.

"Be glad to, Sergeant," John said.

Anti-Aircraft Training

A few days later Sergeant Davis announced that they were going to be shooting again. But this time it would be anti-aircraft training. They would use 22 caliber rifles instead of their 30-30s.

Into the trucks, and off they went. John noticed that he was going a different way from the last trip to shoot. He soon arrived at a field that had a grove of tall pine trees. Each soldier was given two boxes of ammunition (100 Rounds). Teams of four men were formed. They were to lay on their back and shoot at the small wooden planes that were flying through the pines on wires.

John loaded up his automatic 22, lay down on his back, and began shooting. Every time one of the planes came by John, he would shoot it completely off the wire. The instructors stopped all shooting so they could replace the planes. Sergeant Davis began to watch Pvt Dowdy. When the planes began to fly again

John was knocking them off the wires.

"Cease fire!", the Sergeant said. "Private Dowdy," I want you to help me again. We'll teach these 'city boys' how to really shoot.

The only shooting training left was the machine gun and BAR rifles. John did pretty good with the BARs but couldn't get the hang of firing the machine guns. They were too fast for him.

"Going to the movies today," said Sergeant Davis."

John and several of the 'mountain boys' had never seen a moving picture, as they called them. He was all excited. He heard some of the other boys talking about cowboys and Indians. 'westerns', they called them. And there was Mickey Mouse or Popeye.

All of the platoon was in for a surprise. There was no western or Popeye. Lights out, the movie started. "Kill or Be Killed" was the title.

"I thought this was a cowboy and Indian show," John said.

The movie was about how to protect yourself if attacked by an enemy soldier. It showed hand-to-hand combat, bayonet fighting, and other ways of killing the enemy before they killed you.

The movie ended and, the Sergeant went up onto the stage and said, "You had better remember what you saw today. It may make a difference between whether you live or you die. In the next few days we will practice what you saw today."

Combat Training

The next day Sergeant Davis marched the platoon to the parade field and had them sit in a circle. He took his place in the center and said, "I want to see how much you remember about the movie you saw yesterday. Who will be the first to try and put me on the ground? No weapons, just hand-to-hand. Do I have a volunteer?"

He looked all around the big circle of men. "Come on," he said. "Everyone of you will try to put me down before we go back to the barracks."

He pointed his finger and said, "You, private Carroll. We will start with you and continue clockwise until you all have had your try."

Carroll didn't dare refuse, so he got to his feet and walked toward the Sergeant. The Sergeant motioned for him to come on.

"Defend yourself," he said. "I'm going to put your tail on the grass." Suddenly, like lightning had struck, Carroll was flat on his back.

The same thing was happening to everyone who faced the

Sergeant. He put everyone flat on his back.

Then came John's turn. He had watched how the Sergeant had made his move to take advantage of his attackers. He would always take a step to his right before grabbing them. John walked slowly forward. At just the right time, he threw his foot in front of the Sergeants leg as he was stepping sideways. This threw him off balance, and John grabbed him around the waist. He then put what he called the "bear hug" on the Sergeant, his supposed enemy. John squeezed with all his might. The Sergeant threw his arms around trying to break John's bear hug, but he couldn't get loose.

"I surrender," the Sergeant said.

John turned him loose. And backed away.

"Private Dowdy, you are an expert with a gun, and now you show these rookies how to defend yourself. Where did you learn this hug you put on me? This has never happened in the ten years I've been in the Army."

"Well, I did wrestle a little at home. Sometimes with my dad or brother. A few times with our old sow hog when she got out of the hog lot and was rooting in the garden. The only way to put her back was to grab her and sort of drag and roll her along. Don't guess you know how hard it is to hold a hog, do you?"

"Fall in!" ordered the Sergeant. "Back to the barracks. It had been a tough day for him.

As the days and weeks passed, John had done many things that were a new learning experiences for him. He didn't realize that it wouldn't be long before he would be using some of the things he was learning every day. He paid attention to everything, and he learned fast. He would be a good soldier in any outfit he would be assigned to.

John had done well in every phase of his training except the machine gun course. His score was not too bad, but it was not one of the best. He never complained because he was enjoying everything he did. Even his turns at KP and guard duty. He did admit that crawling under the real bullets on his belly with a full pack and his gun cradled in his arms was hard. "If others can do it, I can do it," John said.

When they entered the last four weeks of training, Sergeant Davis had stopped all Saturday and Sunday duties except KP and guard duty. He gave out passes to go off base on Saturdays, but they had to be back in camp by 2300.

John would have liked to go to town, but he had not written a letter to his family back on Little Sam as he had promised. Now would be a good time for him to write that letter. He was ashamed that he had not written, but he had not had time.

John could picture his Dad walking all the way to town and to the Post Office checking for a letter from his soldier son. "No Mail," the postmaster would tell him. Then he would sadly walk away and head back up the mountain.

Charles C. Fletcher

The Letter

Dear Mom, Dad, Brother & Sisters,

First, I want to ask you to forgive me for not writing as I had promised. The fact is, the Army has kept me so busy from daylight to dark every day, and several times we had to go on forced marches during the night. The Sergeant would get us out of bed some times after midnight, and we would march for about five miles and back. The bad part of this is we had to get up at the regular time and stand roll call outside. Getting up at six o'clock didn't bother me. When I was home we all got up about four-thirty or five o'clock every day, so I've been getting to sleep an extra hour since joining the Army.

The marches at night were extra. We marched everyday. It never bothered me, but the city boys had never done much walking, so they complained all the time. I sort of like to go on these hikes. I got to see a lot of things I had never seen.

Mom, I am not sending the money in the mail like I said I would. I'm afraid it will get lost. I have forty dollars. I got forty-two dollars for the two months I've been here, but I spent two dollars at the PX. I bought several orange drinks, some candy and ice cream. I asked if they had any hotdogs, but they said they didn't. I don't think they knew what I was talking about. The base workers seem like they are from some other country. They talk sort of funny. I have a hard time figuring out what they say. And they talk real fast, like they're in a hurry to go somewhere. Never seen no people like that on Little Sam or even in Haywood County.

Dad, you ought to see all the clothes and things they gave me on the first day I was here: toothpaste, toothbrush, bath soap, a comb, two of every piece of clothing -- pants, shirts, underwear (This is clothes you wear under your shirt and pants.)-- handkerchiefs, socks, and shoes. Everything was a little big except the handkerchiefs. They all came in the same size. The summer clothes were tan and the winter clothes were brown. They call them kaki and olive drab. Our work clothes were sort of a dark green. These were called fatigues. I've got more clothes than our whole family ever owned. Must cost our Government a lot of money to have an Army.

Also, I've never dreamed or seen so many things to eat. We have different things every day. We eat three big meals every day except Sunday. Sunday is what they call "cold cut day". I don't mind Sunday's food. It really tastes good. There is cheese, baloney sausage, Vienna sausage, Italian meat, bread, and sometimes pork and beans. For our drink we have cold tea and hot coffee. The baloney sort of tastes like a hot dog tastes, but it is cold, not warm like a hotdog. I don't think you know what all the things I am telling you look or taste like. I didn't at first. I asked some of the city boys and they explained what everything was.

Most of the city boys are good people, but there are a few who think they know everything. They call us boys from the mountains "Hillbillies".

You won't believe it, but everybody takes a bath every day. They don't wait until Saturday night like we do. And they don't have a bath tub. They use a shower. This a pipe coming out of the wall about six feet from the floor. It has something on the end that makes the water look like rain. There are two round knobs with a "H" on one and a "C" on the other. You can make the water as warm or cold as you want it by turning these things. If someone tries to skip his bath, several of the others will strip his clothes off and take him to the shower room and give him a bath. He will never try to go a day without a bath after that.

Have you seen any of the Smiths who live on the next ridge? If you should see that girl of theirs named Sarah tell her I've been too busy to write to her but will the first chance I get. I never noticed her until the night that the Smiths visited before I was leaving for the Army. I walked her home that night and promised I would write and tell her all about the Army. I think she likes me a little bit.

I have heard that we will get off for a week after we finish our training and can get a week's pass to do anything we want to do. I plan on buying me a round trip bus ticket to Canton. I can't tell you the exact day I will be coming home. I'll write and tell you about when to start looking for me. You may not know me when you see me coming up that trail on Little Sam. I'll have my uniform on, and I have got a little bigger in the last three months.

I didn't tell you about the Army barbers cutting all of my hair off right down to the skin on the first day we were here. They cut every one of the boys' hair. I didn't mind, but some of the city boys who had long curly hair that they were proud of, nearly cried when they clipped them. My hair is growing back, but we were told just how long we could let it grow -- not very long.

If something should happen that I don't write about coming home for a few days you could look for me about the first of February.

Tell the girls that if I don't forget I will bring them a surprise when I come home. Mom, I'll bring you some money, and you can go to town one day and buy some of the things you need around the house and some store-bought clothes for you and the girls and maybe a new pair of overalls for Brother and Dad.

If you see the Smiths, tell their oldest boy, Henry, that he should join up as soon as he is old enough. Tell that brother of mine to do a lot of hard work, walk a lot, and practice shooting. He will be old enough in a little less than a year. He had better have Mom help him with his schooling some more. Sure will come in handy.

There are a bunch of things I would like to tell you, but I don't have time to write them all down. I'll try to remember all the things I've seen and all I have learned. I'll tell you everything when I come home.

I miss Little Sam and all the hills and valleys. It's so level here that it looks like the end of the world at a far distance. I miss all of you the most, and I miss my old hound dog too. Hope to see you in a few weeks.

Your Son,

John

Four More Weeks

To John, it seemed like the hard part of the training was over. He was right, things had slowed down -- everything except lights out and 0630 roll call. The platoon was still marching a lot getting ready for what was to be their final "Pass In Review" before the General and all the commanding officers.. This was also a competition to see which company was the best. All the sergeants were trying to get their men in tip-top shape and be the number one platoon.

They had stopped marching to the Mess Hall and could go and come when they wanted. John was usually the first in line, or pretty close to first, at the Mess Hall for every meal. He really loved the Army food. It was lots better than he had back home on the Mountain. This was true for all the soldiers. Things were pretty lean around home regardless of where you were from. The whole world was just getting started on the recovering from the Great Depression of the '30s. Some had more than others, but everyone was poor.

John and all the others were attending a lot of training movies and lectures. There was a lot of talk and guessing about where they would be going and what kind of a outfit they would be assigned to. Everyone was hoping for a some place that they thought they might like, but to John it didn't seem to make a difference. He didn't know much about the world, and any place would be new for him. His only goal was to be the best soldier that he was capable of being. He would do his job like he was told to do.

The last weeks and days of basic training passed fast. The big day for the pass in review parade and the end of training was set for the following Friday. Everyone was getting a little nervous, especially Sergeant Davis. His platoon had helped the company win first place for the last three training groups.

Friday came really quickly, and John was ready to do his part in trying to win for the fourth time in a row. Sergeant Davis did an inspection of his men to make sure they were ready -- shoes shined; neat, pressed uniforms; and everyone knowing what to do.

"Dowdy will be the corner man in the front line," Sergeant Davis said. "He will set the pace, and you all better stay in step with him."

They lined up in formation in front of the barracks and headed toward the parade ground. The review stand came in sight with all the top ranking officers wearing enough medals and ribbons to fill a dump truck. Everyone would be glad when this ended.

The Camp marching band lead, playing some music that John and most of the others had never heard. The parade was on. It was now up to John and the rest of his platoon to do their best.

"Eyes right!" Sergeant Davis barked.

Everyone turned his head. There sat all of the "Brass" watching them strut their stuff.

After they passed the reviewing stand, Sergeant Davis gave

the command, "eyes forward!" They had passed, and another platoon was in front of the stand. John and the others took their place on the field still in formation but standing "at ease".

After all the soldiers had marched by the review stand and taken their places on the field, the officers left the stands to have their meeting to pick the winner. The results would be posted later in the day.

All the units were dismissed and could go wherever they wanted to on the base. John went back to the barracks and changed his clothes.

"These dress clothes are too hot," John said. He changed to his fatigues and went back outside with the others who were waiting for the news from the officers.

They didn't have to wait very long. Soon the company clerk came by to post the results on the bulletin board. Everyone pushed toward the notice to see who was number one. A big yell went up from the ones near the board. "We won! We won number one!"

Sergeant Davis was in the crowd shaking the hands and thanking everyone for the good job they did.

Everyone was told that he could get a week's pass beginning on Monday morning. For those who wanted to go home, a bus would take them to town where they could get a train or bus to wherever they were going.

"You have to be back by next Monday," the Sergeant said. "The orders are being cut for your next assignment. You will be shipped out sometime the next week. Got to make room for the next bunch of rookies. Hope they turn out as well as you have. I'm proud of all of you," he said.

John went to the Sergeant's room a little later that day and said, "Any chance of me getting a pass tomorrow? It's a day's ride by bus, and I have another half day's walk up Little Sam

Mountain."

"Private Dowdy, you have been my favorite rookie. You did everything I asked of you and did it well. I'll see what I can do."

It wasn't long before John had a pass starting on the next morning, Sunday. "The first bus to town tomorrow is at 0700. You can skip breakfast and be on your way home if you want to, the Sergeant told him.

"I sure do", John said. "I'll get everything ready tonight. Thank you, Sergeant Davis."

Charles C. Fletcher

Going Home

John was up, ready, and on his way to catch the town bus at the main gate. He was wearing his dress uniform with all the medals and ribbons he had earned during the different phases of his training. Most of them were earned from the way he could shoot a rifle.

"Just wait until they see me in this uniform," John thought. "Sure wish I had some way of letting them know I'm on my way home. Hope the bus gets to Canton in time for me to walk home before dark."

The bus from camp was on time, and John was at the bus station by 0700. As he was purchasing his ticket he asked the clerk that was waiting on him, "When does the bus leave for Canton, North Carolina?

"One leaving at eight o'clock. The next one is at ten.

"Is there room on the first bus?"

"Sure is. You want to go on it?"

"Sure do. Do you know what time it will get to Canton?"

"Let me see.... Charlotte at eleven; leaves at eleven fifteen; be in Canton around three-thirty."

John was really pleased with this schedule. It would give him time to walk home before dark if he walked really fast.

He found a window seat where he could see all of the strange places that he may have missed when he was going to Fort Bragg three months ago.

The bus was running late when it arrived at Charlotte. The driver had made more stops than usual picking up and letting off people. John was beginning to get a little concerned. Where would he spend the night if he didn't get there in time to climb Little Sam before darkness set in? His only choice was to stay the night at Uncle Tom's corn mill. If he could make it to the top of the mountain, he could go the rest of the way without any trouble. Maybe the moon would be out tonight.

When the bus arrived at Asheville, it was nearly four o'clock in the afternoon. John was getting a little nervous. He new that by the time he changed buses and the bus made a couple of stops between Asheville and Canton it would be late when he got off. He guessed that he wouldn't have time to get home before dark and that he'd have to stay at the corn mill until to-morrow morning.

It was after five o'clock when the bus stopped at the Canton bus stop. After John got off the bus he thought, "If I stay at the mill tonight I will mess up my uniform. The white dust from the corn is nearly an inch thick. It didn't make a difference when I was wearing overalls."

He went into the station. He looked around and said to him-self, "I'll just stay here tonight and get an early start tomorrow morning. I'd better ask if its OK."

He went to the counter where the ticket agent was and asked, "Will it be all right if I spend the night here at the station?"

"That would be all right with me, but I close at twelve tonight. I can't leave you here when I close. Why don't you go up on Main Street to the hotel and get you a room for the night. I don't think they charge much."

"I didn't know that there was a hotel here. Thank you for telling me. I'll go see if they have a room."

Up the street and around the corner, and there it was: "Canton Hotel". He walked up the steps and straight to the clerk who was on duty.

"I need a place to stay tonight," John said. "Do you have a room that I could rent?"

"I sure do," said the clerk. "Upstairs or downstairs," he asked?

"Don't make a difference. How much will it cost me for the room," John asked?

"The price is fifty cents, but we let the men in the Service have it for half price. That will be a quarter for you. You don't get any room service for this price."

"Don't need any," John said. "Just need to have a place to stay until morning, and then I'll be going home. I would go tonight, but it would be dark before I got there, and it's a little dangerous to be walking in the mountains after dark. Could stumble off a rock cliff. Don't want to take any chances."

"Here is the key. Room 106. Just down the hall. If you are going to take a bath, you will have to pick up your towels here.

"Don't think I need one. Took a shower last night at the barracks before I left. Been on the bus all day. Ain't done anything to get dirty. I'll be leaving as soon as it gets daylight in the morning. Where do you want me to leave the key in case there's no one on duty."

"You can lay it on the counter if I'm not up and here."

John gave him the twenty-five cents and started to his room.

"You forgot to sign in," said the clerk. "Everybody has to sign."

John went back to the desk and signed the book, "Pvt. John Dowdy, US Army."

John was up at six the next morning. By the time he got dressed it was beginning to get a little light outside. He had some shopping to do before starting home. He had promised his little sisters a surprise, and they would be expecting it. He went to the Greek restaurant, which never closed. He went in and took a seat at the counter.

The man that who was on duty asked, "What will you have?"

Don't want anything to eat here, but would like to order something to take with me. Do you have any hotdogs?" John asked.

"Don't have any cooked, but it will only take about fifteen minutes to cook them. How many do you want?" he asked

"I want twelve. Could you wrap them one at a time? I'm them taking home with me. Put a lot of chili and onions on them.

"Sure will," said the cook.

"Oh, and can I take six NEHI orange drinks with me? I'll bring the empty bottles back." And would you sell me a bottle of ketchup? Sure makes the hotdog taste better."

"I'll have everything all ready in twenty minutes."

Sure enough, twenty minutes later, the cook came from the kitchen with two big bags.

"Here you are. Hope you enjoy them. I make the best dogs in town. That will be a dollar and fifty cents. Dollar twenty for twelve dogs and thirty cents for the drinks. Don't forget to bring the bottles back," he said.

"Did you put the bottle of ketchup in?" John asked.

"Sure did. I'm not charging you for it. It isn't quite full, but it's enough for twelve hotdogs. And the drinks are really cold. Been on ice for a whole week. Glad to have your business."

John paid him, picked up the two bags, and went out the door headed toward Little Sam Mountain.

As he was walking through the community of Thickety, he heard someone holler at him. He looked around and he recognized the man as the one he sold the hen to four or five months ago.

"Didn't hardly recognize you with them soldier cloths on. You look mighty sharp," he said. "Don't reckon you have any more hens to sell, do you? That hen I bought from you is the best one I ever owned. She never misses a day laying an egg.

"Glad you like her," John said. "When I get home I'll ask Dad if he wants to get rid of any more chickens. Like to stop and talk awhile but I've got to hurry. I've got a poke full of hotdogs and would like to get home before they get cold. I'll stop on my way back to town if I see you out in the yard."

John didn't take the usual short cuts through the woods. He walked in the road leading to the gap between Little Sam and Crabtree Mountain. He left the road and took the sled road up the mountain. He would be home before dinnertime.

Soon he could see the log house. The girls were in the yard playing some kind of game. They didn't see John. As he got closer, one of the girls saw him and screamed, "There's John!" Then here they came, running to meet him. This was a happy moment for John. He loved his family, especially the two sisters. They also loved their "big brother".

The girls grabbed John's arms. "Better be careful," John said. "Got a surprise in these pokes."

John's Mom heard all the loud talking and looked to see what was going on. Then she saw John and started running to meet him.

When they entered the house, John saw that his Mom had started cooking the dinner meal. "Mom," John said, "stop fixing dinner. I have our meal here in these bags."

"What is it?" she asked.

John began laying the hotdogs on the table. He next took out the drinks and the ketchup. "Here you are," he said. "This

is the surprise for the girls and our dinner. It's nearly dinnertime, and it won't hurt for Dad and my little brother Joe to
quit working a little early. One of you girls run out to the corn
field where they are working and tell them that dinner is ready.
Don't tell them that I am home. We'll see what they say when
they first see me."

Betty, the older of the girls volunteered, and off she went.

After a while, John looked out the window and saw his
Dad and brother. They had stopped at the spring and were
washing their hands in the water that was flowing down the
side of the hill.

When they came through the door and saw John they both
were speechless. Hi Dad, " John said". Looks like you and Joe
been working pretty hard. You both are wet . Kind of warm today. John put his arm around his Dad and said. Good to see you .
He then put his hand on his brother Joes'

Shoulder and said. You sure are growing up fast. One of
these days you will be bigger than Dad or me. Mom sure is feeding you well.

John brought our dinner from the restaurant in canton.
It's on the table so if everyone will take there seat I'll ask the
blessing.

Thank you lord for watching after John and keeping him
well. Thank you for this food and all the other blessings you have
given us, Amen.

Everyone sat down and began to unwrap their dinner that
John brought. I got two for each of us . Mom will put the ketchup
on them for you. I'll open the "Big orange" drinks. The man at
the café loaned me this opener. He began to open the drinks. Better not shake them to much. They will spew all over the house.

All the talking and questions had stopped. Everyone was enjoying their treat, especially the girls. Dad was the first to speak

after the eating started. John," He said", This is the first hotdog I've eat in a long time. When your Mom and me were courting we use to get a hotdog every time we were in town. I guess this is why you like them so much. Get it from your Mom and me .Taste mighty good, Thanks for bringing them. The girls hadn't said a word since they began eating. They had finished and were licking the ketchup from their fingers. Did you like the hotdogs, "John asked". Betty, the oldest of the girls said. Shore would like another sometime. I'm so full now that I feel like I'm going to bust wide open.

Don't think I'll be eating any supper.

When everyone was through eating they all went outside to the big shade tree in the yard. Then the questions began.

Did you get to shoot a gun ,"Brother Joe asked"? Lots of times, at least once a week. Nothing to it though. There is this big target that looks like an eye. In the center is a black dot about six inches wide. It's just setting there. I never missed the center. The city boys never hit the wide paper the dot was on. They had never seen a gun.

How is the food," Mom asked"? Never thought I would see this much food at one time. And there is things I have never even heard about. All of it is really good and the dishes never get emp-ty. Bet I've gained some weight?

You haven't shot at anyone , have you, "Dad asked"?

No, but they showed us lots of moving pictures showing us how to kill people. They call them our enemy. The name of the pictures is "KILL OR BE KILLED". Sure hope I never have to kill anyone.

Where will you be at now that you have finished your train-ing, "Mom asked"? Don't know, The sergeant said we would be told next week. I sure hope Bill wolf and me can stay together. I haven't told you about my best Army friend.

He is from Maggie Valley. This is up toward the mountain from Waynesville. He doesn't talk very much. I think his family are Indian. At least part Indian. He said his mom and Dad moved over the mountain from Cherokee. This where all the Indians live.

The men didn't go back to the field. Everyone was enjoying the cool breeze under the tree. Have you seen any of the Smith family lately, "John asked"? No one except the oldest boy, Sam . He was over one day a few days back, Wanted to know when you were coming home. Said his sister Sarah wanted him to ask. Guess I'll go over one day before going back to camp. Sam is about old enough to join the Army. We were talking about it before I joined. Guess he wants to know all about it. He is the only one in the Smith family that I know pretty good. His Mom smiled. She knew better. He was interested in seeing another of the Smiths also.

It wasn't long until it began to get dark. They all left the shade tree and went into the house. They were tired from all that had happened this day. It wasn't long before John said. I think I'll hit the sack. This is what they call a bed in the Army. It has been a long day and I am tired. He began to climb the ladder to the loft where he had slept all of his life. You coming to bed ? He asked his brother Joe. Yep, he said.

I'm a little tired to. Everyone was soon in their bed . Tomorrow would be another big day around the Dowdy house.

The Visit

John was awake when he heard his Mom moving pots and pans around getting ready to cook breakfast. He put his pants on and climbed down the ladder.

"I got to wash up before breakfast," he said.

He took a big pan of water outside, set it on a bench, and washed his face in the cold water.

"Sure is different from the washroom back in the barracks," he was thinking.

He had done this for nearly eighteen years and never given any thought to washing this way. But now he knew that there were other ways to bathe that were easier and better. He dried with the towel that everyone used.

He went back to the loft and finished dressing. When he came back to where his Mom was cooking he said, "Mom, here is thirty dollars. I would have had more, but I had to buy a bus ticket to come home. I'll be mailing you some more later."

He handed her the money and said, "You and the girls go to town one day soon and buy each of you a new dress and some other clothes you need."

"You'd better keep this money," John's mother told him.

"I don't need it. The Army feeds me, gives me my clothes, and doctors me if I get sick. You and the family can buy some of the things you need.

"Thank you, Son," she said as a tear rolled down her cheek.

"I think I'll go over to see Sam today," John told his mom. "I'll be back in a little while. Won't take long to tell him about the Army."

A couple of hours after eating his breakfast John went on his way to visit the Smiths. It would take him about an hour to walk over to the ridge where they lived. Theirs was the only other family that he had known. The people who lived on these mountains of Western North Carolina didn't live to close to each other. They usually lived two or three miles between each other. They didn't visit each other very often.

It was nearing eleven o'clock in the morning when John was close enough to see the Smith place. He was nearly to the house when Mrs. Smith saw him.

"Here comes that Dowdy boy who joined the Army," she said to Sarah, her daughter, who was helping cook dinner.

Out of the kitchen she ran, pulling off the apron she was wearing. She had her hair in a bun and was wearing an old dress.

Mrs. Smith met John on the porch. "My, you sure look handsome in that uniform. Don't even look like the John Dowdy I know."

"Thank you, Mrs. Smith," John said. "Is Sam around?"

"He's out with his dad. I think they went to work in the corn field out back. He'll be here in a little while for dinner. Pull up a chair on the porch. I'll holler for Sarah to come visit with you 'til Sam gets here."

She went into the house and hollered, "Sarah! John Dowdy's

here. Come out and see how pretty his Army clothes are."

Sarah came out on the porch. The apron she had been wearing was gone. She had let her hair down and had a bow tied in back. She also had on her best dress.

"Good to see you, John. I never got any letters from you. Went to the post office three or four times. You said that you would write."

"I wanted to write to you, Sarah, but the Army training kept me so busy, I didn't have time to write anyone. The training is over now, and as soon as I get to wherever they send me, I promise that I will write you often. That is, if you want me to."

Mrs. Smith came out on the porch and said, "Dinner's ready. I see the men folks coming. You and Sarah come in and get ready to eat."

"I'm not too hungry," John said.

"Hungry or not, you come on in here," Mrs. Smith said.

John sat down beside Sarah. The food was passed around, but Sarah and John didn't take very much of anything. After finishing eating a little bit of food, Sarah said, "I think I'll go out on the porch. Don't have much of an appetite," she said.

John hadn't finished eating all the food that was on his plate, but he was eating faster now that Sarah had left the table. He was a little nervous with her sitting by him. He was thinking that she was watching him eat.

"If you will excuse, me I'll go out on the porch with Sarah."

He turned to Sam and said, "When you finish, come out and I'll tell you all about the Army."

"Be right out," Sam said. "Don't lack much. Got to finish off these beans. Too good to leave. Fresh out of the garden, and Mom is the best bean cooker in these mountains. Right, Mom?"

When Sam finished eating, he left the table and went to the porch. There wasn't anyone there John and Sarah had left.

"Wonder where them two could be?" Sam said.

He left the porch and began searching for them. He wanted to hear about the Army. One more year, and he would be old enough to sign up. He finally located them sitting under the big shade tree up next to the spring. He started toward where they were when his Dad hollered from behind, "Time to go back to the field. You ready, Sam? Got to finish up there today. Got to do some fence mending tomorrow. That old cow has got out twice and when milking time come, I liked to never find her."

Sam turned around and headed back to the house.

"Guess I'll see John later. He'll be home all this week," he said.

John and Sarah were sitting side by side and talking about the future. About what they would do when John finished his Army duty.

"Your mom sure is a good cook," said John. "Sure hope you can cook like her."

"My mom can really cook good. Guess it comes natural for the woman of the house in these mountains to be good cooks. They can make a good meal out of nearly nothing and stretch it so there will be enough for everyone. I help Mom cook all the time," Sarah said. "She's always bragging about what a good cook I'll be someday..

They talked about lots of things that each had done since they saw each other. John told about the Army and Sarah about what all she had done around the house and what she saw when she went to town to check if there was a letter form him. The afternoon went faster than John or Sarah wanted it to pass.

John was quiet for a few moments and then looked straight at Sarah. "Sarah," he began. "If you really want me to I will promise again that I will write you a letter as often as I can. Until you came over to my house that night before I left for the Army I had never give you a second look when I came over to visit Sam. I'll admit that I think you are a pretty girl and I want to be your good friend if it's all right with you."

Sarah looked toward John and said, "John, when you came to see Sam, you didn't know it, but I would peep out window to see you. I've liked you for a long while. Hope you never forget me. You know what? I'm not a little girl anymore. I'll soon be sixteen years old, come my next birthday. I haven't seen many boys: your brother, Sam, and you. Oh, I did see lots of them when I went to town. They didn't pay any attention to me, and I never looked at them twice. I don't think I would like any of them city boys. They tell me that they are smart alecks and don't treat their wives too good. No sir, don't need one of them. I'll marry me a mountain boy and move off this mountain someday."

Sarah finally hushed talking, and John said, "You know what, I kind of feel the same way as you do. I think I want a mountain girl for my wife. And I'll never live on this mountain after I get out of the Army."

"Sarah," John said, "when I come back from the Army, I would like to ask you to be my wife, that is, if you don't find someone else.

"I'll wait," Sarah said. "I wont quite be an old maid. I'll be a little over eighteen. Don't want to wait much longer. When you get old, no boy wants to marry you. I promise, I'll wait if you will."

The long-term engagement was made. They talked a little longer and then John said, "I'd better get home before dark. Could get lost. Been three months since I've crossed that ridge. I'll come over again before I leave. Got to go back on this coming Friday."

They both stood up, put their arms around each other, and John said, "I think we love each other."

He removed his arms from around Sarah, said good-bye, and

headed toward home.

He never gave any thought to not telling Sam about the Army. His visit was really about what he had done today: see Sarah and spend some time with her. The visit with Sam was put on hold.

The week was going by fast for John. He spent a lot of time with his mother talking about the past and what the future might be.

"Did you and Sam have a good talk the other day? she asked.

He looked off in the distance for a few seconds, turned toward his Mom and said, "You know what? I didn't talk much with him. He and his dad were pretty busy working in their corn field. They said they had something that they had to finish that day. Never did hear the what it was . Saw him a few minutes at dinner time while we were eating. Tomorrow is Thursday, and I don't leave until Friday. I'll go over tomorrow and visit him."

John left early the next morning headed toward the Smith house. He wanted to see Sarah again and visit with Sam and tell him all about the Army. When he arrived at the Smith's he saw Sam at he spring house. He met him on his way back to the house carrying buckets of water from the spring.

"Hi, Sam," John said. "I come over to visit you and tell all about the Army if you have time."

"I'll be right back," he said. "Soon as I set this water on the porch."

"I'll wait," said John.

John and Sam went back to the shade tree near the spring. "Sorry I didn't get to talk with you the other day," John said.

"That's OK," Sam said. "Looked like you and Sarah had a lot to talk about, anyway. Dad wanted to finish with the corn so he could go to town the next day. He never was one to put off anything. Never happy until he finishes a job once he starts."

"How old are you, Sam?" John asked.

"Be eighteen on my next birthday. That is in December. Why do you ask?" Sam said.

"Well, let me tell you a little about the Army. I think it's a great place. They give you three meals a day: breakfast ,dinner and supper. I never ,in my life saw so much food. And they feed you things that you never saw in your life. Don't know the name of all that they feed me, but everything tastes good.

"And when they gave me my Army clothes, there was two of everything: two pants, two shirts, and more socks, and what they call 'underwear' and several handkerchiefs. Never had a handkerchief in my life, nor underwear either. And to beat it all, they give you two sets of everything. One for summer when it's hot and another set for the cold winter. You get a big sack that they call a 'duffel bag'. You put everything in it after rolling or folding it the way they teach you. You get a back-pack that has half of a tent, a rain coat and some other things in it. There is a short-handle shovel strapped on the outside. You get your own gun that you have to clean every time you take it outside, and you have to learn to take it apart and put it back together behind your back.

"They sure keep you busy, but it's a good place to live. I bet you would like the Army. You can join after your next birthday. Better think about it."

All the time that John was talking to Sam, he was looking toward the house. They had talked for a short while when John noticed that Sarah was sitting on the porch.

"Is there anything else I can tell you about the Army," John asked Sam.

"I guess not," Sam said. "I think I'll look into joining up after my birthday. Everything you told me sounds great."

"Guess I had better speak to Sarah before I go," John said.

He left Sam and walked to the house where Sarah was waiting for him. "Hi Sarah," got time for me to visit with you?"

"Sure do," she said. "In fact, I've been looking for you this morning. Are you going back to the Army tomorrow?"

"Yeah," he said. "I've got to sign back in on Sunday. I'll take the bus back on Saturday. Don't want to mess-up. I get along real good with my Sergeant, and don't want to make him mad. Do you still want me to write to you?" John asked Sarah.

"Sure do," she said. "Hope you do better than the other time you promised? I never got the first letter, not a one."

"Things will be different now that I have finished my training. I'll have a lot more free time to do the things I want to do."

They talked for about what the future might hold for them and what they would be doing until they met again.

"See that high ridge over yonder," John said. "There is a big grassy field on top of that ridge. That's where I'm going to build our house. You can see for miles from up there. On a clear day you can see Canton and the paper mill as plain as day. Yes sir, there is where we are going to live. Lots of good farm land up there, too."

Sarah said, "I hope you don't stay away too long. I'll walk up there one day soon and pick a spot for our house."

Soon it was time for John to head for home and get his clothes packed. He would be leaving really early the next morning.

They put their arms around each other, and this time John kissed Sarah on the cheek. It wasn't a real kiss. Just a peck of a kiss. Neither of these new lovers had any experience at making love. In time this would change.

"Better get home," John said. "Got a lot of packing before bed time. Don't want to do it tomorrow morning. Got to get an early start toward town. You take care of yourself, and I'll write every chance I have."

He took his arms from around Sarah, turned, and headed for the trail going up the ridge toward his house.

After arriving home, John spent the rest of the evening with his family. They talked about what all they had done since John left for the Army. John told them again about what he had been doing.

"Mom," John said, "why don't you and the girls walk with me to town tomorrow morning? You could shop around a little, we could get a bite to eat at dinner time, and you could be back home before dark. How about it?"

"Don't think I can go. There's dinner to fix for your dad and Joe. And besides, my best clothes need washing and ironing. Better stay home this time. Me and the girls will go one day soon. Then your dad and Joe can eat leftovers from breakfast for one day. They need to lose a little weight anyhow."

John looked at the clock on the mantle above the fireplace and said, "It's nearly nine o'clock. "We'd better start getting ready for bed. Don't want to stay up too late. Been a pretty busy day for me. How about the rest of you?"

John and Joe climbed the ladder up to the loft where they had slept as long as they could remember.

John said, "I think I'll sleep in a pair of my old overalls. Don't want to get any wrinkles in my uniform. Want to look clean and neat when I get back to camp. Needs to go to the cleaners soon anyway."

They lay on the straw ticks that they used for mattresses and talked for a little while. Then Joe fell asleep. John lay there thinking back through the many years that he and his brother had slept in this loft and about how they found snow that had blown through the gaps between the logs onto their beds and about the times when they woke up in the morning to find all kinds of birds and small animals that had crawled or flown through the cracks trying to find a warm place. Sometimes the nights were bitter cold in the winter months. Neither he nor his brother had ever complained about their "bedroom". It had been all that they knew. John now knew better. The Army had given him a soft cot to sleep on. While he had been the Army, never once did he see any snow or animals when he woke up in the morning.

John thought that he would never come back to live on Little Sam, especially in this house. He had seen another world since joining the Army. He took a deep sigh, turned over on his side and fell asleep. He needed rest for the bus ride tomorrow.

About four o'clock the next morning he was awakened by the crowing of their old red rooster. He must have known where John was sleeping because he had left his usual roost and was perched on a limb in the tree that was at the end of the house where John was sleeping. This made John mad. He was used to sleeping until six every morning. This rooster was two hours early.

"If he wouldn't go to bed so early, he wouldn't wake up so soon. He gets on his roost as soon as the sun goes down," John muttered. "Oh well, John said. I'll be gone in a little while, and he can crow his head off. I'll be gone, and he will still be here."

When John heard his mother in the kitchen getting everything in place to start cooking the family breakfast he pulled, off the overalls that he had slept in and dressed in his uniform. He climbed from the loft, went outside, and washed his hands and face. He didn't have to comb his long black hair like he used to. The Army had taken care of that for him. His hair was growing back, but he had kept it cut really short. He liked it this way.

Back in the kitchen with his mom he said, "Are you sure that you can't come with me to town this morning?"

"No, I'd better not. I can't just walk off at a minute's notice. There're things to be done before going anywhere. That is, unless all the family goes. Then you don't have to have meals cooked for the ones who stay at home. Better not this time," she said again.

It wasn't long until all the family was up and about. They might have heard John and his mother talking, or they may have smelled the ham she was frying. They didn't eat ham everyday: only on special occasions. It was one of those special occasions this morning.

John always said that his mother was the best cook in all of these mountains. She could make anything taste good by the way she would cook it. And talk about biscuits -- nobody could outdo her. She patted them out with her hands. They were about the size of a saucer. You'd split them apart, put a big piece of fresh churned butter in between, pour some homemade sorghum syrup over them, and you had a meal fit for a king. The Army fed John well, but they couldn't make biscuits like his mom, and he craved them every now and then. Nobody cooks like the women in the southern part of the United States, especially the ones who live in the mountains of western North Carolina. This is where you will find the best cooks in the world.

Mrs. Dowdy put the food on the able and said, "Breakfast is ready. Everybody get to the table."

They all took their regular places where they had sat for every meal. Mr. Dowdy asked for the blessing of the food, and then everyone began passing food around the table. It was kind of like what John did in the Army: you'd get some food and pass it on to the next person.

John's mother was the last one to take her seat. She had to get the last pan of biscuits from the oven and put them on the table. It didn't take long for the first batch to be gone.

After everyone was finished eating, they all left the table and went into the sitting room. John began to get all of his belongings together for the trip back to camp.

"Good to have you home, son," his Dad said.

Joe spoke up. "Don't worry about the work around here. Dad and me can keep it up."

"What surprise are you going to bring us the next time you come home?" asked the girls.

His mom began, "John, you didn't stay long, but it was nice to have you with us again. It's hard to see one of you children leave home, but I understand. When you get to a certain age you want to go on your own. Why, even the birds and all animals go and leave their mother when they can take care of themselves. I'd better start cleaning up," she said.

John noticed tears coming from her eyes as she turned and went into the kitchen.

"May be back Christmas," John hollered to his mom.

"Dad, why don't you check in town about a job and move off the mountain? I hear talk that the government has jobs for most anyone who wants to work. It's called 'WPA' or something like that. They say it pays fifty-cents an hour. That would be twenty dollars a week. Pretty good pay, I think. Even the paper mill is hiring a few people every now and then."

"I'll think about it. Be pretty hard to leave this peaceful mountain and live in a noisy city. I'll let you know about it if I do decide to move off the mountain."

John put his cap on, picked up his duffel bag, and went out the door. He looked back to see all of the family, except his mom, standing on the porch watching as he headed down the trail toward town. After a ways, he looked back and all of them were still on the porch. He waved once more and never looked back again.

"It has been a good visit," he said.

Back To Camp

It didn't take as long to go off the mountain as it did to climb it. John was soon in the settlement at the foot of the mountains where the houses were not far apart. He looked for the man who bought the chicken from him a few months ago. Must have been a little early for him to be out and about. John didn't really want to see him anyway. He wanted to have enough time to visit Uncle Tom at the corn mill before going on to town.

It wasn't long before he was in the road that ran along the river bank. The river came out of Cold Mountain and others in the Pisgah chain of mountains. John headed straight to the corn mill located on Beaverdam Creek near where it entered the river. The water from this creek supplied the power to run the machinery in the mill.

As soon as John entered the mill, Uncle Tom saw him. "Well, I wish you would," he said. "If my eyes are seeing good, it's that soldier boy, Dowdy. How are you young man?" said Tom.

"Getting along just fine. Been home for a week. Got all my Army basic training done. Would have stopped to see you on my way home, but it was Sunday, and I knew you didn't work on church day. Want to thank you again for telling me about the Army. They must have a lot of money the way they give you clothes and things. Don't know where they buy them. Never seen any in the clothing stores in Canton."

"Glad you like the Army," Tom said. "Wish I had stayed when I was in. I wouldn't be grinding corn now. No siree. The Army has a good plan so when you stay for the required time you can retire and draw a pension the rest of your life. They would have lost money on me. I have lived longer than most men. Getting way up there in age now. The good Lord has been good to me, and I thank him for this long life."

"Got to go, Uncle Tom. Hope you are still around when I come home again. I'll never forget the times you let me sleep in the mill. Sure helped me out."

With his duffel bag over his shoulder, he headed straight to the Canton Hotel. "Better get me a room before they are all rented. Need a place to sleep tonight. I want to catch the eight o'clock bus so I will be back to camp before dark on Saturday."

When he entered the lobby of the Hotel and went to the desk to sign in, there was no one there. He noticed a little silver bell and a sign that said, "Ring Bell for Service". He touched the bell, and nothing happened. He looked it over real good and gave it a lick with his hand: "Bing-Bing".

Here comes someone. "Well, what do you know? You did come back."

John was surprised. It was the same man who was there when he came home. "I need a room for tonight," John said. "Do you have one I can rent?"

"Sure do. You can have the same room you had the last time if you want it."

"That would be fine," John said.

"Here is the key. Sign the guest book, and that will be twenty five cents."

John paid him and went to his room.

It was one o'clock, and John was getting a little hungry. It had been a long time since he had eaten. "I'll go around the corner to the Greek café and return the Nehi drink bottles he let me take home."

He got the bottles out of his duffel bag and left the hotel and headed toward the eating place.

When he entered, there wasn't anyone behind the counter. He set the bottles down and said, "Anybody here?".

Someone came from the kitchen, and when he saw John, he said, "Well, if it ain't that soldier boy again. See that you brought the bottles back. I knew I could trust you. It would have cost me twelve cents for them if you didn't return them. Want anything to eat?" he asked.

"Guess I better eat something. May get a little hungry before tomorrow. I think I'll have a couple of hotdogs. Don't know when I'll get another. Did you know that they don't sell hotdogs in all the cafes? Just here in Canton, I guess. Be sure to put lots of onions and chili on them."

It was about ten minutes when he brought the hotdogs and set them in front of John. "Want anything to drink?" he asked.

"Guess I'll have a Nehi orange if you have any."

"Coming right up," the cook said.

"Oh, do you have any ketchup?"

"Here you go," he said as he handed John the bottle of ketchup..

Didn't take John long to finish off the two dogs. He got a napkin and wiped his mouth, then said, "How much do I owe you?"

"Well, being you are a soldier and don't get paid very much, and you are a good costumer, this meal is on the house."

"Thank you," John said. "Mighty nice of you. I have money. The Army pays real good. I get nearly twenty-one dollars every month. They take out nearly two dollars for some kind of insurance. I guess they have to hire someone to bury you if you die or get killed.

"Back home, when someone dies, the church bell will toll and all the men-folks get their shovels and mattocks and head to the church cemetery. They know there is a grave to be dug. Someone who is a pretty good carpenter will make the box to put the dead person in. When everything is ready for the funeral, everyone will gather at the church at the foot of the mountain. One of the church men will read from the Bible, the congregation will sing a couple of songs, and the box with the body will be lowered to the bottom of the grave with ropes. Some of the men will shovel the dirt and throw it in the grave until it's full to the top. All of this doesn't cost anything. No need for insurance.

"Probably come by in the morning real early and eat a bite. At least enough to hold me until I get back to camp. You will be open, wont you?"

"We never close," said the cook. "I'll probably be here. Come on by, and I'll fix you a good breakfast."

John got up from the counter to leave and said, "Thank you for the eats. See you tomorrow."

He left and went straight to his room at the hotel. After a good bath he went straight to bed. He was tired. Been a long day for John.

John was up before daylight, getting dressed and packing all of his belongings back into the duffel bag. He would take everything along with him to the café that was located on the way to the bus station. This would give him more time to eat breakfast.

No one was at the desk in the hotel, so John laid his room

key on the counter where the book was that he signed when he rented the room the night before. There was a blank piece of paper laying beside the book. "Why not leave a thank you note?" John said. After all, they did let him have the room for half price. "May have to stay here again sometime. Uncle Tom at the corn mill said to me once, 'Son, there is an old saying I heard years ago that I have practiced all my life: You can catch more flies with a grain of sugar than you can with a pound of salt.' This has worked for me for many years. Never hurts to be good to people. Never know when you will have to ask a favor from them."

John picked up the pen and began writing, "Dear hotel man, I can't think of words to tell you how much I thank you for your kindness for letting me stay here when I needed a place to sleep. I hope I can come here again. (Signed) PVT John Dowdy, US Army."

This was the best John could do with a thank you note. He had never done much writing. "At least this will let them know I appreciated them," he said.

When he entered the café, there was no one around. "They must spend about all their time in the kitchen," John said. "Anybody here?", John hollered.

"Be right with you," someone said. When he came from the kitchen and saw John he said, "Didn't know if you would get up early enough to come by for breakfast. What would you like."

John had very little experience of ordering food. The times he had eaten in a café, he'd always ordered hotdogs. He wasn't about to eat dogs for breakfast, so he said, "What do you usually serve your customers at breakfast time? he asked.

"Well, for you, I think a couple of eggs, some bacon, grits, toast, and a cup of coffee. Could add some 'saw mill gravy' if you want it."

"Sounds good to me," he said. "I think I'll have the gravy, too."

"Be about ten minutes," said the cook.

John was familiar with everything he was having for breakfast except the 'saw mill gravy'. "Never heard of this kind of gravy," he was thinking. "I've eaten white flour gravy. Must be some kind of city gravy."

When the cook set everything before John, he said, "If this don't fill you up, let me know and I'll fix some more. I got to get back to the kitchen. I'm getting things ready for the dinner meal. Always a big crowd. Lot's of the men come over from the paper mill. Seems that they like our food better than bringing a lunch from home. Glad to have them."

He went back to the kitchen, and John looked his breakfast over. This gravy looks just like the kind Mom makes every morning. I guess this fancy name helps sell it."

He began to eat his breakfast, and everything tasted good to him. As he was eating the toast, he was thinking, "Shore wish I had some of Mom's biscuits instead of this toast."

He finished eating and hollered back to the man in the kitchen, "I've finished. If you will come and let me pay you, I'll get to the bus station."

He came from the kitchen, went to the cash register, and said, "That will be twenty-five cents. Not going to charge you for the coffee. "That's on the house. Sure you had enough to eat?" he said.

"Sure did. Thanks for the coffee. Better get going. Don't want to miss the early bus. I'll come by when I get to come home again. Got to have another one of them hotdogs you make. You sure know how to cook them. See you," John said.

The bus was right on time. Eight o'clock on the nose. The driver took John's duffel bag and put it in the storage place under the bus. John got on and took a seat near the front. He noticed that there were only six other people on the bus.

"They must be from Waynesville where the bus started from."

By five minutes after eight they were on the road heading toward Asheville. If there was someone along the road who waved for the driver to stop, he would pull off the road and let them on. John was in no hurry like he was on the trip coming home. He didn't mind the stops.

When the bus pulled into the station in Asheville, the driver said that everyone going to Charlotte could stay on the bus if they wanted to. It would be about fifteen minutes before the bus would leave. John didn't get off. He didn't want to lose his seat should there be a lot of other people getting on for the trip to Charlotte. Sure enough, after everyone was on, there wasn't a vacant seat. In fact, there were other people wanting to go on this bus but there wasn't any room for them. They would have to get the next bus which would be leaving at ten o'clock.

As they left the mountain area, John was not missing any of the scenery. The farther they got away from Asheville, the leveler the fields were. The buildings, barns, and houses were all larger and were built in a different style from those in the mountains. Also, John noticed that there were poles with wires tied to them all along the road. Everyone in the flat land must have had electric lights and telephones. The only people who had these back where John lived were the people living in town.

John sort of went into a trance from watching all the telephone poles fly by, and he dozed off for a nap. He was wakened from his short nap by the voice of the driver.

"Everyone will be getting off when we reach the station in Charlotte. That's as far as I go. There will be an hour's wait before the bus leaves for the coast. If you are going to Fort Bragg, you will take this bus. Good to have you with me today. Hope you enjoyed the trip."

The bus pulled into its parking space. The driver stood by the door until everyone was off. He then opened the door to the baggage section and unloaded all the suit cases, boxes and, John's duffel bag.

He picked up his bag and went into the station. "What will I do for the next hour?" he was thinking. "Better not go too far from the station. Could forget the way back and be late. Don't want to miss my bus. Got to be back at camp before 24.00 tonight. That's when my pass ends. Better not leave my bag sitting around. Someone could pick it up or I could forget it. I would hate to go to the Supply Room and ask them for some more clothes. They have already given me more than I need. Ain't never dreamed of having so many shirts and pants, not counting all the other stuff."

He found him a good seat where he could see all the people coming and leaving the big bus station. He never saw anyone that he knew, but he was getting an education watching and seeing all kinds of people, fat, skinny , short, tall, old, young, pretty, and ugly. John never realized that there were so many different kinds of people. He even saw a couple who looked like they were from some far-away land. They had a towel or something wrapped around their heads. Sort of odd looking people.

"Attention," came the voice over the speakers. "Bus number eight now loading at dock number two for all points south going to Wilmington. Please have your ticket in your hand when getting on the bus. It will be departing in ten minutes."

John picked up his duffel bag and hurried to the loading dock. He wanted to get a good seat by the window so he could see the country. He handed his ticket to the man at the door of the bus.

"I need to have you put my bag somewhere," John said.

The man took John's ticket, took a tag from his pocket, and tied it to the bag. He tore off the bottom with a number on it and handed it to John.

"This is your claim ticket," he said. "Put it in a safe place. You will need it to get your baggage when you get off. Next."

The bus was about half loaded when John got on. There were plenty of good seats to choose from. He picked a window seat where he would be near the side of the road. He didn't want to miss seeing the way the people lived in the "flat land" area.

John made the trip to his home on Little Sam Mountain and back to Fort Bragg. He didn't have any trouble other than the arrival at Canton too late to get home before dark. Everything worked out for John. He had spent a night in a hotel . This was a first for John. He had turned in his pass and was now in his barracks getting everything unpacked and back into his footlocker.

Back on Duty

It was time for supper, and John was hungry. The last meal he had was the breakfast at the Greek Café that morning. The Sunday meal was usually cold cuts, but this was fine with John. All the food was different from what he was raised on, and he loved all of the different kinds of food that the Army fed him. He washed his hands and headed to the Mess Hall.

On the week-end they got their food cafeteria style. Only through the week did they get their food served to the table by a KP. John went through the line and found a table all to himself. He sort of liked some privacy every once and awhile.

He got seated and started to eat when someone said, "Mind if I join you, Dowdy?"

He looked up from his food and saw who it was. "Sergeant Davis," he said. "I was hoping that I would see you. I looked for you at the office when I turned my pass in. Wanted to let you know that I was back on time."

"Knew you would be," said Sergeant Davis. "Dowdy, I want to have a talk with you tomorrow morning after I get all the men assigned to their duties. Now don't get nervous and stay awake tonight thinking something bad is about to happen. I can tell you this much. It's about your future service in the Army. You have a great opportunity to better yourself, and I want you to get that chance. Get a good night's sleep. See you in the morning." With this Sergeant Davis left.

John finished his meal, went back to the barracks, and sat on his bunk. He couldn't keep from thinking about what the Sergeant had said. "Oh well. As Mom used to say, 'Always do your best, and the good things will come to your door.'"

The people of the mountains had many sayings, some for the good and some for the bad things. It seemed that John's Mom knew all of them and believed that they were true.

"Going to bed. Forget about what will happen tomorrow, and make the best of what happens. Good night, Bill," he said to his friend from Maggie Valley. "I'm pretty tired from the bus ride, and think I'll turn in early. See you in the morning."

At exactly 06:00, the lights came on in the barracks, and Sergeant Davis let out a war yell. "Everybody up and at 'em.

Reveille and roll call in thirty minutes. Shake a leg."

Everyone hit the floor just like they had been doing for the past three months. They dressed as fast as they could and went out in the street in front of the barracks.

Here came Sergeant Davis in full uniform. "Fall in," he barked. He began calling the names of the men in his platoon: "Adams, Baker, Carlton, Dowdy," on and on all in alphabetical order.

Soon he finished and said, "Get them bunks made before going to the Mess Hall for breakfast. Can't tell when some of the Brass will drop in. They are trying to decide where all of you will be going for permanent duty now that you have finished your training. Sure going to miss you guys. You have been one of the better bunches that I have had. Haven't give me too much trouble. Dismissed."

John walked slowly to his bunk. His mind was thinking of what the Sergeant would want to talk to him about. He made his bunk, went to the Mess Hall, but didn't eat the usual big meal that he always did. He couldn't keep from thinking about the meeting with the Sergeant. He finished eating, got up from the table, and went back to the barracks.

Sergeant David was giving orders to all the soldiers in his platoon. When everyone had been given a job he said, "Ready to go, John?"

"Yes Sir," John said. May as well get it over with. Let's go."

"At ease, Dowdy. It's nothing bad like you are thinking. You are in for a big surprise that you may like."

The Captain

Sergeant Davis and John headed for the section of camp where all the officers had an on office. They entered one of the buildings and went to a desk where there was a soldier with a patch on his arm that said, "T5".

"Tell Captain Pugh that Sergeant Davis and Private Dowdy are here. He is expecting us."

The Soldier got up from his desk and walked to the door that had a sign on it that read, "Captain Pugh". He knocked on the door and a voice said "Who's there?"

"Sergeant Davis to see you, Sir. "Send him in," he said.

They removed their hats and entered the office. The Captain stood up behind his desk, raised his arm and returned the salute that John and Sergeant Davis had given him.

"At ease," he said. "Have a seat, and we will get down to business." They all sat down, and the Captain began to talk.

"Private Dowdy," he began. "Sergeant Davis brought it to my attention what a good soldier you are. I have an offer for you to consider. As you have seen by now, we are in the business of making soldiers out of boys like you. We need all the help we can get, and good, dedicated men are hard to find. Sergeant Davis would like for you to stay with us as a part of the training team. He would like for you to help him with the next group of trainees. If you want the job it is yours. I will also put in for you to be promoted to Private First Class."

John didn't speak for a few moments and then said, "Sir, my best friend, Private Bill Wolf, lives pretty close to me back in the mountains. We are always talking about staying together if we can. Is he being shipped out?"

"I'll have to check the orders. Sergeant Davis, could you use another person to help you? You did mention Wolf when we were talking about this the other day. I can always use more help. Private Wolf is also a very good soldier and nearly as good on the firing range as Dowdy."

"Yes, I would like to have him, also. I didn't want to be 'hoggish' when I asked for some help. Getting two good men would be a blessing for me."

"I will do anything you and Sergeant Davis want me to do," John said to the Captain. "It don't have to be, but it would be nice if Bill stayed at this camp. You do what you want to do. I think it was real decent of you to ask me. I know you didn't have to ask. You could have ordered me to stay, and that would have been it. Thank you, Captain."

John was using the old saying, "a grain of sugar".

"I'll let you know sometime later today."

They all stood. The Captain said, "Dismissed". They exchanged salutes. John and Sergeant Davis left the room.

When they were outside and on their way back to their barracks, Sergeant Davis said, "Thank you, Dowdy. You and me will work the buts off the next bunch. They will be real soldiers when we get through with them. I'll let you know about Wolf as soon as I find out . Hope he gets to stay with us."

When John got back to his barracks there was no one there. Everyone was still wherever the Sergeant sent them earlier that morning.

"Guess I'll hang around until dinner time. Everyone should be back by then. Sergeant Davis is supposed to give the orders to the men telling where they will be going for step two of their Army life. John already knew where he would be for the next three months. He was pleased with this assignment, and if Bill got to stay, it would be great for both of them. And to beat it all he was getting a promotion. "This will mean that I will be getting more money every month. Don't know how much, but lots more than I had back on Little Sam."

All the men came back in time to wash up for dinner. Everyone was excited and talking about where they might be going. John didn't tell them what had happened this morning. "Best to keep it a secret until the Sergeant announces it along with the other orders."

John was a little hungry because he didn't eat very much breakfast from thinking what was to happen when he visited the Captain. He would make up for what he didn't eat this morning.

When Sergeant Davis returned to the barracks, John was standing near the door. "Good news, John," he said. "The Captain had Bill Wolf's orders changed, and he will be staying here and working with you and me. We'll show the next bunch of rookies what real training is."

When all the men were back from the Mess Hall, he told them to be in front of the barracks in fifteen minutes. When all the men were out of the barracks, Sergeant Davis had them fall in to formation. "When I call your name," he began, "fall out and form a group."

He began to call out names, and they stepped out to the side into a group away from everyone. There were about twenty in the first bunch.

"You are group number one," he said. "You stay together."

He continued calling names until there were five groups.

"Group number one," he continued. "Have all of your belongings together by 08:00 tomorrow. Take everything but your gun and the sheets and blankets on your bunk. Leave the gun in the rack. Fold your bedding and leave it on the foot of the bunk. There will be a bus here to pick you up to take you to the train station in town. There will be someone put in charge of your group who will have the orders for your new location. Don't ask me where you are going, because I do not know. The Brass make these decisions, not me."

He continued to give times and orders to each group. When he finished, he said to John and Bill. "Let's go to the PX and have a beer."

When they were seated, the bartender asked, "What will you have?"

Sergeant Davis said, "I'll have a big mug of beer. What do you two want?"

John and Bill looked at each other for a few seconds and, John said, "Neither one of us have ever drunk any drinks with alcohol in them. Do you mind if we drink something else?"

"Good for you. Beer drinking is a habit just like smoking. Once you start, it's hard to quit. I never started smoking, so that's one bad habit I don't have. I've noticed that you don't smoke either. Order anything you want to drink. They're on me. Sort of a celebration of my good luck getting you two as helpers for the next three months.

The bartender was still waiting for Bill and John to order.

John spoke up, "Do you have any 'Nehi' drinks?"

The bartender sort of smiled and said, "You mean them big bottles of soda water that look like they're orange?"

"I guess that's them," John said.

"Coming right up," he said.

It didn't take him long. In two minutes, he was back with a big mug of beer and two bottles of orange "dopes". Want a glass for the pop, he asked? No. 'druther drink them out of the bottle. Don't spill any this way. The bartender smiled again and moved on to the next customer.

New Recruits

It was a week before the next group of soldiers arrived. All that Bill and John had done for a whole week was sit around, eat, and sleep. Sergeant Davis had taken a week's leave and gone home to Tennessee. John didn't know if he was married or not. He never talked about his family.

John did manage to write a short letter to Sarah and his family. He told of the plans to stay at Fort Bragg for another three months and about his going to get a promotion and more money. The letters were more like long notes. He did promise to do better the next time. He told them that he was very busy, but things would lighten up now that he had a new job. He did mention how much he loved them and how he missed them.

Sergeant Davis was back on Sunday before the new men arrived. He asked Bill and John to come to his room at the end of the barracks. "John," he said. "There is a room at the end of the room down stairs. You can move in there if you want to. And there is a room on the other end on this floor that Bill can use. Of course you will have to make your bunk and keep everything neat and orderly just like you always have been doing. This is sort of a 'perk' of being on the training staff."

Bill and John didn't have to be told any more about their new living arrangements. They were on cloud nine. This was something that they had never had in their life: a room of their own.

The next morning when John and Bill came back to the barracks after breakfast, Sergeant Davis was waiting for them. "There will be another bunch of new recruits coming some time after lunch. I am giving you your first job as members of the training instructors. When they arrive I want both of you to meet them as they unload from the bus. John, there will be one of them who was put in charge while on their way here. You get the folder from him. It will have the names of who we will be getting. Have them fall into formation, and as you call their names, have them form another formation. When you finish calling the roll, march them to the Barber Shop. John, you make sure that they go in the Barber Shop, and, Bill ,you stand at the door on the other end of the building and check to see that they got their haircuts. Then line them up. When the last one gets his haircut, march them here to the barracks. I'll tell you what to do next after I have finished talking to them."

Zimmerman

The bus arrived about 14:30. When they were all off the bus and lined up for roll call, John began calling out their names. "Adams, Brumfield, Cooper, Dover," and on down the list of names that were in alphabetical order.

When he came to the name "Zimmerman", no one answered. John called the name a few times more and asked, "Anyone know this Zimmerman?"

One of the boys raised his hand and said, "Sir, he sat in the seat beside me until we stopped for lunch, but he never got back on the bus. The driver waited for about ten minutes and said he couldn't wait any longer."

John made a note of one man missing, made sure all of the men got their haircuts, and then marched them to the barracks.

Sergeant Davis was waiting for them. He started his speech the same as he did when John first met him. "My name is Brad Davis, but while you are here you will call me 'Sergeant Davis'. Is that clear?"

No one answered.

"I can't hear you", he said. "Do you understand what I said?"

Still no one said anything.

"I'm going to tell you once, and only once. When I ask you for an answer, I expect an answer. If I don't get an answer, you will pay for not giving me one. Do you hear me?"

"Yes Sir!", they all said.

"That's better," said the Sergeant.

PFC John Dowdy and PVT Bill Wolf are my assistants. During this training period they will be helping me with all the different things that we will teach you. You will give them the same respect as you give to me and do whatever they say the same as you would do if I told you. They are both experts at the things you will be doing. As long as you obey orders and give me the best that you have, we will get along fine. If I catch you goofing off, you will pay a price. I hope we will be good friends when all of this is over."

"John, show these men where they will be sleeping while here. After they choose their bunks, take them to the Supply Room. You and Bill know what needs to be done for the rest of today. Good luck, men," Said Sergeant Davis. I'll go check on our lost soldier.. Got to put the MPs onto him. I have never lost a soldier, and don't expect to lose Zimmerman. He will be here before the sun goes down tomorrow."

Saying that, off he went. John and Bill would have these new men for the rest of the day. Sergeant Davis would be helping the MPs find Pvt Zimmerman.

After everyone had claimed a bunk, John had them fall out and get into formation. "Follow Pvt Wolf. I'll bring up the rear. Got to hurry. Won't be long until chow time. I'm sure you all are hungry after what you have been through today. We feed pretty good at our mess hall. Left face," John said.

Then came his was his first problem as a leader. It so happened that the new men didn't know what John wanted them to do. Some turned right, some left, and others stood still.

"The first lesson I'll be giving you will be about how we talk, Army talk, and what it means. But at the moment we are going to the Supply Room where you will get the clothes you will be wearing as long as you are a soldier. Just follow Pvt Wolf."

Bill was standing at the door where the recruits came out after getting all of their clothes and other supplies. "Go back to the barracks and put your clothes in the foot locker at the foot of your bunks," Bill said. "When everyone gets back from the Supply Room, we will all go to the Mess Hall for supper." I don't know what we will have to eat tonight. The Mess Sergeant always has something different, and he keeps it a secret from us soldiers.

When they were all back in the barracks, John said, "When I tell you to 'fall out', it means that I want you to go outside and stand in front of the barracks. When I say, 'fall in', I want you to form two lines with the same number of men in each line. 'Left face' means for everyone to turn left. You do the same if I say 'right face', only to the right. 'Forward march', means you go forward. There is a lot more that I will teach you starting tomorrow morning. Now, 'fall in ... left face ... forward march.'"

They went off to the Mess Hall behind Bill who was leading the way.

That evening before lights-out, Sergeant Davis had John and Bill come to his room. "Well, the MPs are trying to track down Zimmerman, and I received the schedule for the three month training. The 'Brass' up at headquarters work these things out. They have to because there are several thousand soldiers here, and we all can't be on the rifle range at the same time. We will use the rest of the week teaching them how to line up in formation and how to keep in step when marching. Everywhere they go for the next three months they will be marching. Better get a good night's sleep. Tomorrow is going to be a long, tough day for us as well as the new soldiers. Sure hope they locate Zimmerman. Good night. See you at roll call tomorrow morning."

John and Bill went straight to their rooms and were in bed before Sergeant Davis hollered "lights out".

The next morning after breakfast when all of the platoon were back in the barracks, Sergeant Davis divided the men up into three groups. Dowdy, Wolf, and I will show you what to put into your backpack and how to pack it. You will carry this on all hikes and lots of other times that we are in the field. The total weight, including your rifle, will be about seventy pounds. May seem heavy at first, especially for all you city boys, but you will get used to it."

Packing the backpacks continued all morning.

"When you get back from lunch, we will go to the parade field and learn a little about the proper way to march. Better eat a lot. It's going to be a long afternoon," Sergeant Davis said.

When everyone had returned from the Mess Hall, Sergeant Davis called John and Bill to his room. "Good news," he said. "The MPs found Zimmerman back at the place where the bus stopped for lunch. When I finish my lunch I'm going over to the MP office and get him. John, you and Bill take the men and start the training. I'll get back as soon as I can."

"No problem," John said. "Bill and I can handle them until you get back."

Sergeant Davis took Zimmerman into one of the rooms at the MP Office. He sat behind a desk and had Zimmerman sit directly in front of him.

"Zimmerman, I want you to tell me what happened after you had lunch and why you never got back on the bus. You had better have a good reason or you could end up in the stockade.

You took the oath of a soldier when you enlisted, and that made you a full-fledged US soldier. In fact you have been AWOL. OK. I'm listening."

"Well, Sir," Zimmerman began. "After I finished eating my lunch I decided to go to the restroom before getting back on the bus. I picked up a newspaper lying on the lunch counter and went to the toilet located at the back of the café. I found the sports page and began reading about how the Dodgers were beating the Yankees in the World Series. I forgot about the bus and kept reading until I finished the whole paper. Then I realized that I was supposed to go back on the bus as soon as I finished eating. I threw the paper on the floor, pulled up my pants, and headed out to where the bus had parked. The bus was gone. I didn't know where it was going, so I couldn't start walking and hoping I would get a ride and catch up with the bus. All I could do was wait and let someone find me. And that's the truth, Sir. The Dodgers are going to win the World Series, I think."

Sergeant Davis looked down at the top of his desk for a few seconds and then looked Zimmerman straight in the eye. "Zimmerman," he began, "I've heard all kinds of stories and excuses from recruits, but the one you just told me is the grand-daddy of them all. And do you know what? I believe you. From this day on while you are in my outfit you had better forget about the Dodgers and any other baseball team. I'm going to make it as easy as I can on you, but you will start your Army life in the Mess Hall peeling potatoes, washing dishes, and cleaning floors for your first week. If you have anything you need to bring along, get it and let's get out of here."

"Yes Sir," he said. "Do you like the Dodgers? he asked Sergeant Davis. He didn't get an answer, only a mean look.

Before joining John and Bill, Sgt Davis took Zimmerman for his haircut and to the Supply Room for all his GI clothes. After he showed him where he would be sleeping and having him put his clothes away and change into his fatigues, Sgt Davis took him to the Mess Hall and introduced him to the Mess Sergeant.

"This is Pvt Zimmerman," he said. "You can have him for the rest of the week. Tell him the hours that he is to work, and don't be too easy on him. Let him see what happens to anyone who messes up in my outfit."

"Sure will," said the Mess Sergeant. "He will get your message."

Sgt Davis left the Mess Hall and went to join John and Bill. He would tell them about Pvt Zimmerman that night after supper. "What a way to start a new training cycle," he thought.

By the end of the week, all the drill instructions were pretty well learned, and the marching was getting better. Zimmerman was nearly finished with his Mess Hall duties and would join the outfit on Monday. Over all, with the help of his two assistants, Sergeant Davis was moving along at a pretty fast pace.

"Sure wish I had asked for some help before now," he said. "Lucky to get two good men like Dowdy and Wolf. One of these days they will be the two best soldiers in the Army."

Hiking

When everyone was back at the barracks after breakfast, Sergeant Davis told them to get their back packs ready. Today would be their first hike.

"Pvt Wolf, you help Zimmerman. He hasn't been instructed. All his Army life so far has been in the Mess Hall. Time for him to catch up with a little hard work and some extra time."

The Sergeant continued, "Dowdy will be in charge of the hike today. I have some paperwork and a visit to the Captain's office to do. Got to get this Zimmerman thing behind me. I'm trying to keep it off his records as being AWOL. Don't want any criminals in my outfit.

"The chow truck will bring lunch to you at noon. This is a pretty long hike, and if you move it, you will be back in time for supper. You will obey Dowdy's and Wolf's orders the same as you would mine. And if you don't, you will pay for it. See you tonight."

The "hikers" were soon on their way. They were divided into two groups: half on the left side of the road and the others on the right side. PFC Dowdy was leading them and Pvt Wolf and the truck with the water and first aid supplies were at the rear. Dowdy was setting a pretty fast pace, and the "city boys" who had never done any hiking were getting pretty tired. Dowdy noticed that they were struggling and dragging their feet.

"Company halt!" Dowdy hollered. "Take five, smoke 'em if you got 'em."

He didn't have to tell them twice. Everyone found a place to sit on the bank beside the road.

The five minute break was soon over and Dowdy said, "Fall in! Forward march!"

They soon reached the half-way point and had lunch from the chow truck that arrived on time at twelve o'clock.

"Time to start back to camp," John said.

The march back to camp was a lot faster. The men were tired and wanted to get back to the barracks, take a good shower and hit the "sack". This was only the first of many cross country marches that they would make before they finished their training.

Everyday was a surprise for the new recruits. They never knew what they would be doing until they came back from breakfast.

Gas Masks

"Today," Sergeant Davis began. "We will have classes and show you the importance of your gas mask and how and when to use it. This is very important for you to pay attention to. This is the only time you will have the opportunity to have this training. What you learn could possibly save your life someday, so pay close attention."

They were taken into a big building where they were shown films on how to put the gas mask on in the shortest time. There were also films showing soldiers having to use their masks. They also showed what happened to those who didn't get their masks on the correct way or didn't get them on at all. The results were scary although the scenes were by professional actors and all "make believe".

Then practice of putting the mask on was repeated over and over for about an hour. "Put you mask back in the case like it's supposed to be," said Davis. "Got to get back to the barracks. Nearly dinner time."

When everyone had his gas mask hanging around his shoulder and was ready to leave, someone hollered "Gas attack! Gas attack!".

No one had noticed the sprinkler heads on the ceiling. This was where the gas was coming from. It looked like smoke or a deep fog. Some of the men had no trouble getting their masks on. The ones who had trouble were rubbing their eyes and coughing as they tried to get the masks on. There was only a little gas and it stopped. This was a part of the lesson on how important the gas mask was.

Every phase of the training went well for the next few weeks. Even Zimmerman was catching up, and he seemed to like the Army life. He hadn't mentioned baseball any more. The Sergeant had got his message through to him. With help from John, Zimmerman had became an expert shot with the 30-30 rifle. He earned his Marksman medal. With help from John and Bill, every recruit in the platoon was a qualified rifleman.

The training was about to come to an end. "Going to do one more thing before graduation," said Sergeant Davis.

Camping Trip

"We are going on an all night bivouac," Sgt Davis explained. "'Bivouac' is what you call a 'camping trip' back home.

"Everyone will take his full pack including sleeping bag ,shelter half, and poles. We will march to the area where we will pitch camp. Each of you will have to choose a buddy to share your tent with. He will have half of the tent and you the other half.

"Everyone is to be packed and ready to go at 08:00 tomorrow morning. All of the company brass will be at camp. They will ride, not walk. All of us will walk, including me. Do any of you have questions?"

At eight the next morning, not only Sergeant Davis's men, but everyone in the whole company were going, all four platoons: A, B, C, and D. Also, all the company officers were going to be a part of this outing. They were to grade each one of the platoons on how good their training had been. There would be one winning platoon.

After everyone was in formation, John and Bill inspected every man to make sure he had everything he was supposed to take with him. One of the company officers gave orders telling in what order they would march. A Platoon went first followed by B, C, and then D. This meant that John's platoon was at the tail-end of the march. There were lots of trucks and other vehicles that were leading the way. Also, an ambulance was at the rear.

They arrived at a very large field with pine trees scattered about. Each platoon had a color assigned to its area. D platoon was red. They were given red arm bands to wear all the time that they were in camp.

It was nearly dinner time when everyone arrived. The trucks that were to be the mess hall along with the cooks were all set up for feeding everyone. There were also latrines and showers in tents that had been set up sometime before. Everyone was expecting to have to "rough it". This was a first-class camping trip.

The recruits experienced another first. Their food was put into their mess kits and coffee into big aluminum cups. After everyone finished eating lunch, everyone teamed up and pitched their tents. John and Bill had done this during their training, so they were the first to finish.

Next came digging a foxhole by each tent. Again, John and Bill had no trouble finishing first. Some of the men had a little trouble. The ground was mostly sand, and they would throw out one shovel and two would slide in.

When all the holes were dug, everyone was given a break to catch his breath. The rest didn't last long for some. They were walking around to see who their neighbors were.

Sergeant Davis, John, Bill, and all the officers knew something that the rest of the company didn't know. John and all the others who were not trainees each had a can of gas. At a pre arranged time they took up positions assigned to them. They all opened their cans, threw them down and hollered "Gas! Gas! Gas! Gas!" Then they put their masks on.

Some had their masks with them like they had been instruct-ed, but most of the men had left their masks in their tents. They were running every where looking for their tents and masks. When some of the men opened the carrying case candy, ciga-rettes, and other stuff fell out.

Zimmerman had the most trouble. He kept pulling sports magazines out trying to get to his mask. All the time his eyes were watering, and he was screaming, "I'm dying! I'm dying! I'm dying!"

There was not enough gas to hurt anyone. It was just enough to teach them to always keep their gas masks with them as they had been told.

Sergeant Davis had himself a good laugh while watching Zimmerman. When everything was back to normal, Pvt Zim-merman walked over to where Sergeant Davis was standing.

"Sergeant Davis", Zimmerman began. "You told me to forget about baseball and the Dodgers. I tried to, but I did a little sneak-ing around. I didn't think I would be caught. I should have done what you told me. I promise you from this day on the Dodgers and all baseball are in my past. They could have been the cause of my dying."

Sergeant Davis smiled, looked Zimmerman in the eye, and said, "You are going to make some outfit a very good soldier."

Zimmerman hung his head and went to his tent.

After a night of sleeping on the ground, a half cold breakfast, taking the tents down, and packing, the company was ready to hit the road back to the luxuries of the barracks. Marching back seemed a lot shorter, and they didn't take as many breaks as they did on the trip the day before. The lunch break didn't take up much time. The meal was cold cut sandwiches.

When they arrived back to the barracks, the first thing after laying their packs on their bunk and placing their guns in the racks, they headed for the shower room. After a shower and clean clothes, they were ready for a nice hot meal.

The parade before all the brass to see which platoon was the best was held the last of the week. This was the last part of their training before shipping out to some company that would train them for whatever they would specialize in on the battlefield.

Mystery Meeting

Sergeant Davis asked John and Bill to come to his room after they finished their supper. He wanted to talk with them. John asked what it was about. The Sergeant just said he didn't have time now but that it was nothing bad.

"Wonder what it could be?" Bill asked.

"Don't know," John said. "Must be something important. He never has us in his room unless he wants to talk about the training. Not going to let it stop me from eating," John said. "I'm as hungry as a bear. That field food and the cold cuts didn't last long. After all the walking and other work, a body needs some real food."

John and Bill went to the Sergeant's room at the end of the barracks. John knocked on the door.

"Who is it?" Sergeant Davis said.

"It's Bill and me. You said that we were to come after we finished eating."

"Come on in. The door isn't locked."

They opened the door and went in. Sergeant Davis was sitting on his bunk. "Over there are a couple of chairs. Have a seat. Won't take long to say what I have to tell you."

"While we were out in the field yesterday, the Captain sent his runner to tell me he wanted to see me. I went to his tent. They had the big tents. He had me sit down, and he began talking."

"Sergeant Davis," he began. "I've been watching the two men who have helped you with this training cycle. I believe their names are PFC Dowdy and Pvt Wolf. What do you think about the way they take hold of the assignments given them?"

"They are two of the best men I have ever worked with. Never have to tell them twice when I want them to do something. Yes Sir. Real good men."

"I Want you and them to come to my office after the parade on Friday. We will be there within thirty minutes after I dismiss them at the parade."

"That all, Sir?"

"Yes, Sergeant, thank you for coming. See you Friday afternoon."

"So now you know as much about what he wants to see us about as I know. I have told you word for word what went on between the Captain and me. Wish I knew more to tell you. And I would sleep better if I knew what he has on his mind. Seems that all officers like to keep their secrets and surprise you when they tell you something. I like our Captain. He is a good company commander. All the men under his command are like his children. He takes care of them."

Before Friday afternoon came, Sergeant Davis, John Dowdy, and Bill Wolf had many thoughts run through their minds as to what the Captain wanted to talk with them about. There were many, many things that each of them were asking themselves. Some good, some bad.

"Shore wish it was Friday," John said to Bill.

"Me too," Bill answered.

"I don't think we have done anything wrong that would concern the Captain."

"Can't think of anything," Bill said.

"I think if we had messed-up, the Captain would have had Sergeant Davis on the carpet, and he would have been on our backs," John told Bill.

The parade was over, and D platoon had won again. Sergeant Davis was happy, and it was the big day John and Bill had waited for all that week.

Sergeant Davis was already at the building where the Captains office was when John and Bill arrived. "Well men, are you ready for our visit with the Captain?"

"Sure am," John said. "Waited all week for this meeting. Want to find out what it's all about."

The Meeting

Sergeant Davis said to the Corporal who was at a desk outside the Captains office, "Tell the Captain that Sergeant Davis is here as requested."

He pecked on the door before opening it. "Sergeant Davis here to see you, Sir."

"Send him in," the Captain said.

"Go on in, he is expecting you."

The three entered, raised their arms and saluted the Captain. He returned the salute and said, "At Ease. Have a seat."

As he sat back down behind his desk, he said "Would you like a little drink before we get started?" He pushed a little button, and the corporal came in. Bring us four glasses and some ice and soda water."

"Yes Sir," he said.

"If you are talking about drinking whiskey, I don't think I'll have any. Saw a bad thing happen back home one time. My Mom said it could happen to anybody. Thank you just the same, John said.

The Captain leaned forward and said, "What was this thing you saw?"

"Are you sure you would like to hear about it, Sir? Take a little time to tell you."

"I've got time," he said.

"Well, I was about ten or eleven years old at the time. It was on one of the coldest days of the winter of 1935. Dad and me were outside all day cutting wood for the fire. When we went back to the house, Dad started coughing and said he was feeling poorly. Must have caught a cold. As soon as we ate supper, he went straight to bed. Said he was freezing.

"The next morning he said, 'John, how about going over to the Ledbetter's and ask Rufus to send me a jar of his moonshine. I've heard that it will cure most any sickness.'

"The Ledbetters lived on the back side of the mountain toward Beaverdam. When I got to Rufus's house and told him what I was there for, he pulled out a box from under the bed and handed me a jar of whiskey he had made.

"'Dad said he would pay you when he got some money,' I told him.

"'Ain't no charge. Glad to help a sick neighbor.'

"When I got back home Dad poured out a milk glass full of Rufus's medicine, put in a little sugar, some ginger powder, and drank the whole glass full."

John paused for a moment.

"Go on, go on," said the Captain. "What happened next? The Captain was all ears. John was doing a good job telling about what had happened.

"Well, in about ten minutes Dad began to act sort of funny like. Mom got up from her seat before the fireplace and was about to put her hand on his forehead to see if he was running a fever. Dad jumped back, ran out the door and across the yard to the apple tree. He climbed as high as he could and hollered out, 'They can't get me now.'

"Mom begged for him to come down and get in the house out of the cold. He didn't budge an inch. Stayed in that tree for nearly two hours and finally come back into the house. Mom fixed two glasses of buttermilk with raw eggs stirred in them and had Dad drink them. He headed straight to bed and was asleep in five minutes.

"Mom had all us children gather around and said, 'Now you have seen what drinking will do to you. I hope that none of you will ever touch that stuff.'

"And I have never drunk anything with alcohol in it."

"Did he get well," asked the Captain?

"Sure did," John said. "Don't know if it was the moonshine or the buttermilk."

The Captain turned to Pvt Wolf and said, "How about you?"

"Well, Sir, my dad was a full-blooded Cherokee Indian. I know you have heard that an Indian goes wild when he drinks. So, if you don't mind, I'll pass, too."

"What would you two like to drink, then?"

John spoke up and said, "A 'Nehi Orange' drink would be fine."

The Captain pushed the button again, and the corporal came in. "Bring two orange drinks from the icebox. If there is none go to the PX and get two."

"Yes Sir. Right away."

Soon everyone was enjoying his drink. The Captain and Sergeant Davis with their bourbons; John and Bill with their Nehi Oranges.

The Captain took a big drink, wiped his mouth with his hand and began. "I know you all are hearing about the war in Europe. The war has caused an increase in young men joining military service. There has been such an increase here that we are having to form another company. When this happens we will need more people to train all these new men. I'll get to the point as to why I had you come to my office.

"PFC Dowdy, Pvt Wolf, Sergeant Davis has recommended to me that you two would make good platoon Sergeants for a couple of the barracks. I agree with him, and if you would like the assignment, I will get you both promoted to the rank of Sergeant. What do you think about it?"

John spoke first. "It's an honor to be offered the job and promotion. I'll do what ever I am asked to do, but from the day I signed up I have wanted to go to some infantry company and train to be a foot-soldier. I have always been outside, done a lot of walking, and don't think I would be as happy here as I would be in the infantry. But, I'll do whatever you want me to do."

"How about you Pvt Wolf?"

"Sir, I feel the same as John about the Army." As you know, Indians love the outdoors. But I'll do whatever you want. Thank you, Sir, for your trust in me."

The Captain didn't say anything for a few seconds and then said, "I could order you both to stay here and take these jobs. I thank you for giving me your honest answers. But I'm a little surprised at your turning down the promotions. I think you will be two of the best soldiers in the US Army regardless of where you go. I'll transfer you to the best outfit that I can find. And I guess you two want to stay together? Good luck to you, and thank you for helping Sergeant Davis for the past three months."

He stood up and everyone else did the same. He saluted and said, "Dismissed".

Back at the barracks John said to Bill, "What do you think? Did we turn down a good deal when we asked the Captain to send us to an infantry outfit? We would have had it easy here, and besides that, we would be getting a promotion that we may never get in the infantry."

"Well," Bill said. "I don't know about you, but I had rather be outside and be a private than be cooped up here doing the same thing over day after day, month after month, and maybe the rest of our lives."

"Guess you are right. Don't think I would be happy to stay here forever."

Hotdog Lunch

Sergeant Davis stopped by where John and Bill were sitting outside the barracks. "John, I remember that every time we go to town and stop at an eating place you nearly always ask if they have any hotdogs. You also told about the hotdogs you have back home. What is the name of the café that makes the hotdogs you are always bragging about?"

"It's the only big restaurant in Canton. It is owned by a Greek family, and they stay open 24 hours a day. The name is 'The Greek Café'. Why do you want to know about the café?"

"Well, thought I might stop there and check out them hotdogs you are always bragging about. That is, if I ever pass through your town. See you later," Sergeant Davis said as he walked away.

On Saturday morning the Sergeant told John and Bill that he wanted them to eat lunch with him. Today is cold cut day, but I wanted to have one more meal with you two before you leave here. You will probably get your orders to ship out about Monday or Tuesday."

"We will be ready," John said. "What time?"

"Twelve-thirty will be fine," said the Sergeant as he left.

The two young boys from Western North Carolina didn't think about it being unusual to get a special invite from their Sergeant to eat with him. It had never happened all the time they had been at Fort Bragg.

When they reached the Mess Hall, the Sergeant was standing by the door waiting for them. "Right on time," he said. "I think the Mess Sergeant is about ready to feed us. Come on in and we will find us a table."

They didn't stop in the dining room where John and Bill usually ate. He led them to where the officers ate. They felt a little uneasy when they realized where they were.

"Everything is fine. I reserved this place for a couple of real fine soldiers. Be at ease; everything is fine. The food will be here shortly."

They went to a table near a window and sat down. The door opened, and the Captain and his orderly came in and sat down at the table with the Sergeant, John, and Bill.

"Davis said that he had ordered a special meal for you two and wanted me to be a guest. I brought along my right-hand man. He likes to eat, too."

John and Bill were getting a little nervous from the presence of the Captain and his Corporal. John noticed that on the table next to where they were sitting there were a couple of boxes with something written on them. He moved over a bit so he could see what the writing on the box said. He saw the words "Nehi Orange". "What is going on here," he thought.

The door from the kitchen opened and out came the Mess Sergeant and a couple of KPs. They began setting pots and pans of food on the table. Before long John knew what the "special meal" was. There was no mistake about what they were having for lunch: hotdogs. There were a big pot of chili, a dish of chopped onions, mustard, ketchup, and a big flat pan of steaming hotdog buns.

When everything was on the table, the Mess Sergeant said, "Let me tell you all about what you have for lunch. Well, Sergeant Davis asked me to fix something special for two soldiers who are leaving us. I asked him for a suggestion as to what it might be.

"He thought for a few minutes and then said, 'I know the perfect meal.'

"I asked what it was, and he told me, 'hotdogs a la montagnes -- ones just like Dowdy is always talking about.'

"'Never heard of them,' I told him.

"He said, 'Boil some weenies and set mustard and onions on the table and the men will make their own hotdogs. Also, call the Greek Café in Canton and get their recipe.'

"I called the café, and the cook remembered the soldier who bought the sack of dogs and carried them home to his family. He told me, step by step how to make the chili, cut the onions, and how long to boil the weenies. Even told me how to wrap the buns in a damp towel and steam them so they would be fresh."

The Mess Sergeant then set plates before everyone, got the Nehi drinks and set them on the table, and said, "Enjoy your hotdogs, men. If you need anything more just give me a call back in the kitchen. Got to go feed the rest of the men. Leave a couple for me," he said.

The hotdogs tasted just like the ones John ate at the café in Canton. "Think I'll have another one. Only ate three and drank one Nehi," John said.

The others were also on their second or third hotdog. "Sure glad that I was invited. These are the best hotdogs I have ever eaten," said the Captain. "May have them served to the whole staff one of these days. I'm sure that most, if not all of them, have never eaten a meal like this. I'm about to bust. Three is my limit. If you'll excuse me, I'll get back to the office. Got to get some paperwork in order for a couple of men who will be leaving us next week."

Everyone stood up, but there was no saluting. The Captain left the dining room and headed back to his office.

"Wish I had asked him where we were going," John said to Bill."

"Wouldn't have done you no good," Sergeant Davis said. "That's one thing the Army does and does well. They keep you in the dark as to what's going to happen until the last minute. Guess they have a reason."

John stood and looked toward his Sergeant and said, "This is the kindest thing that has ever happened to me in my whole life. Thank you, Sergeant Davis. I hope I don't disappoint you in the kind of a soldier I become in the future. Thank you for my favorite food." He turned his head to hide a tear that had come into his eye.

"Better get back to the barracks. Got a little more packing to do. Don't want to wait until the last minute, and you can never tell how soon you are to leave once they tell you. I'll cut through the kitchen and thank the Mess Sergeant and KPs for fixing this special meal for us. See you all later he said as he left the table."

New Assignment

Early on Monday morning right after breakfast, Sergeant Davis went to John's room. He pecked on the door and called John's name. "You home," he asked?

"Sure am. Come on in. Door's not locked."

Sergeant Davis opened the door and said, "John, I saw the Captain at breakfast, and he told me to have you and Bill come to his office sometime before lunchtime. He didn't say he had your orders for transferring ready, but I bet that is what he wants to see you about. When you get back, look me up and give me the low-down on what he wanted. That is ,if it's not classified as a secret."

"I'll do that," said John.

It was nearing 10:00 when John said to Bill, "I guess the Captain has had his morning coffee by now, so let's go and find out what he wants."

"Guess so," Bill said.

They went in the office where the corporal's desk was. "Tell the Captain that Privates Dowdy Sand Wolff are reporting as requested."

The orderly knocked on the door and went in. When he came out he told them to go on in. The two soldiers went in , stood at attention, and saluted the Captain. He returned the salute and said, "At ease. Find a chair and sit down. This won't take long, but no need to stand up. No need to offer you a drink because I know you both will refuse.

"Got good news," he began. "I called my old company commander who I knew when I went to OCS. He was a Captain then, but was promoted several times since I saw him. He is now a full Colonel and commander over a whole infantry division at Fort Benning, Georgia. Fort Benning is not only the best infantry training center, but also the largest one in the United States. I had a good talk with him and explained that he could get two of the best soldiers that we have had here at Fort Bragg in quite some time. He said to send them on down. He also said that they were growing so fast that with all the volunteers joining the Army, they would have to start a new company. It would be great for him to get someone like you two.

"They'll be looking for you some time this week. He had Captain Brown call with all the details. Captain Brown called and, gave me a phone number for you to call when you arrived, and he will look for you on this coming Thursday. I have your orders in this envelope with the phone number on the front page."

He handed the envelope to John and said, "Still time to change your mind and stay here. That's it men. I wish you a lot of luck, so I'll say 'good-bye.'"

They saluted each other, and John and Bill turned to leave the office. They didn't reach the door before the Captain said, "Private Dowdy, you didn't tell what your Dad did with the rest of that mean moonshine. Did he finish drinking it?"

"No sir, he hasn't touched a drop of licker since that day on. You wouldn't want to hear what Mom did with it. Probably take five minutes to tell you the whole story."

"I've got five minutes to spare to hear what happened if you have five minutes to tell me."

"Not much to tell, but if you want to know, I'll tell you. After Dad had that wild spell, Mom poured the rest of that jar of moonshine in the slop bucket on the back porch. She keeps this five gallon bucket to save the scraps of food in to feed our hogs. The next day when she went to the hog lot to feed the old sow hog we kept, she didn't think anything about the licker in the feed bucket. She poured the full bucket into that old sow's feed trough and she ate and drank it in nothing flat. Mom went back to the house to finish her morning cleaning. Wasn't long when she heard the old hound dogs barking their heads off. She looked out the window and couldn't believe what she saw. That old sow had pushed the fence down and was out in the yard chasing the dogs. That was one happy hog. It came to Mom as to what was happening. The sow was drunk from her breakfast of bread scraps and moonshine.

"'Better leave her alone until she sobers up,' she said to Dad when he came to the window to see what the dogs were barking at.

"That's it, Sir. Are we free to go now."

"You're dismissed," said the Captain. "If I am ever up in that part of North Carolina, I'll make it a point to find this man named Ledbetter."

Sergeant Davis was waiting for John and Bill when the got back to the barracks. "Well," the Sergeant said, "care to tell me what the Captain had to say?"

"Sure," said John. "He pulled a few strings and arranged for Bill and me to transfer to the top infantry training base in the world."

"Don't' tell me you two are getting to move to Fort Benning down in Georgia."

"That's the place we are headed for. We have to leave this coming Thursday. I have the orders here in this envelope. The commander over the infantry outfit is a friend of our Captain. They became friends when he was taking officer's training at Fort Benning. Guess it pays to know the right people."

"Are you going on the bus, or will you be taking the train?" the Sergeant asked.

"The Captain said we would go on the train. He gave each of us a voucher to pay for our dinner. What is a voucher?" John asked the Sergeant.

"Oh, it's sort of like a check only it has what it can be used for."

"Never had any checks, what are they like?"

"If you put your money in a bank, they give you a little book that has blank pieces of paper where you can write how much money you want to give someone and sign it. They turn this in at the bank and get their money."

"Sure sounds like a lot of trouble. I had rather use plain old money. Got to go now. See you later."

John and Bill went to their rooms to see about finishing packing, and the Sergeant went toward the Captain's office. He was glad to get away from teaching two mountain boys about the banking business.

The next morning, Sergeant Davis had John and Bill come to his room. "Good news, men," he said. "You will not have to ride the camp bus to town and get a taxi from the bus station to the train station. I checked with the Captain about taking you two to the train station. He said it would be OK for me to check out a car from the motor pool and take you."

"That's great," John said. "Would have been sort of a job getting on and off the bus with all our belongings. You shouldn't have gone to all this trouble for two Privates."

"Glad to do it, and beside that, I'll have a day off and have my own car."

"I never drove a car," John said.

"Me either," said Bill.

"Won't be long until you will be driving. One of the first things you will be learning is how to drive any type Army vehicle. Everyone has to know how to drive in case a driver should be killed. You or someone would take over."

"Not many cars back home," John said. "If I owned a car I could never get to my home. The only way to get from the Crabtree road to our house is to walk. When we take corn to the mill, we use a one horse sled. Have trouble with it sometimes. The road up the side of the mountain is steep and narrow. Talked to Dad about moving the family off the mountain to town. Said he may, some day. I don't think I'll ever make my home on Little Sam."

John and Bill were up early Thursday morning and went to the Mess Hall for breakfast. The Sergeant was already eating when they went in.

"You two ready to go," he said.

"Will be as soon as we finish eating. All our stuff is at the door back at the barracks. Ready to go."

"I picked the car up last night," said Sgt Davis. "Full tank of gas and ready to go. Not very often that I get to take a car off base. What time do you catch the train?"

"Nine o'clock. The Captain said something about changing trains when we got to Atlanta. Said a different train went to Fort Benning. We've never rode on a train. Is it better than the bus?" he asked the Sergeant.

"I think so. On the train you can get up and walk around, but on the bus you sit in one place until it stops and lets you get off. Get to see a lot of pretty things, too. Goes through the countryside that's not covered with billboards advertising all that stuff for sale. Yes sir, think you will like the trip. Better hurry up. Getting close to 08:00, and it takes thirty minutes to drive to town."

As he left the Mess Hall he said, "I'll have the car at the barracks door when you get there."

The Train Ride

They were at the train station twenty minutes before their train was due to leave. John went to the ticket window and gave the tickets to the clerk. "Is there anything I need to do before getting on the train?" John asked the clerk.

"No, everything looks good. The conductor will take the tickets once you are on your way."

A porter loaded John and Bill's duffel bags in the baggage car and gave them a ticket stub so they could pick them up when they arrived at Fort Benning. The conductor said, "All aboard! All aboard!"

Sergeant Davis, John, and Bill shook hands and said goodbye. "Lots of luck to you," said the Sergeant.

They boarded the train and found a good seat near a window. The car was about full. Most of the passengers were soldiers going home or to a military base like John and Bill.

The conductor waved a lantern, stepped into the coach, and closed the door. The train began to move. They were on their way to Fort Benning Sand a new adventure.

The railroad ran through the countryside and open spaces. Sometimes it would be miles before they saw a house or car. Nothing but peach orchards, cotton fields, and several kinds of wild animals as well as horses, mules, goats, cows, and occasionally a few sheep. The scenery was beautiful from the train. Not like on the bus where you saw lots of houses, factories, cars, and advertising signs along the road.

The train move faster than the bus and had fewer stops. The conductor went into each coach and announced that if you were going to certain places you would have to change trains in Atlanta. Fort Benning was one of them.

"Atlanta sure is a big place," John said.

"Sure is," said Bill. "Hope we don't get lost and miss our next train."

They gathered the things that they were carrying with them and were ready to get off as soon as they stopped.

"Be sure that you take all of your belongings," the conductor said.

"Guess we'll eat lunch when we get on the other train," John said.

"Sure hope so. It's nearly lunch time."

The train had stopped, the doors were opened, and about half of the passengers got off. Most of them were soldiers.

"Probably going to the same place that we are. Guess we better ask the man at the ticket window about where we are to get on the next train. Pardon me," John said to the man behind the booth. "Where will I catch the train that is going to Fort Benning?"

"Let me see your ticket," he said. He took the ticket from John, looked at it and said, "Your train is at Gate 12. It is loading now. Better run along or you may miss it and the next train for Fort Benning is at 6 o'clock this evening."

John grabbed his ticket and asked the direction to Gate 12. The ticket man pointed to his left. John and Bill headed in the direction that he pointed looking for a number 12.

"There it is," Bill said.

They got in the line in front of the number 12. "Hope they don't get a full load before we get there," John said. The line was moving very slowly, but they got on the train and found good seats.

They were soon moving out of the Atlanta station and on their way to their new home. After everyone was settled down the conductor announced that lunch was being served in the dinning car. "Which way?" John asked.

"To the back car. Be careful when you go from one car to the next. Hold to the hand chain. It's three cars back from here."

He didn't have to say anything more. They were on their way for dinner. "Got to remember to tell the family about this the next time I write home. Eating while riding about fifty miles an hour. Hope they believe me."

When they entered the dinning car, a porter met them, led them to a table, and handed each a menu. "You gentlemen decide what you want and I'll be back and take your order."

"Got any hotdogs on this list," John asked.

"No sir, 'fraid we don't. There are a lot of sandwiches and soups to choose from. I'll be back."

"What are you eating?" John asked Bill.

"Don't know. Never had to make choices; just et what Mom set on the table. Don' know if I will ever get used to the way city people act and live. Don't have a problem at the mess hall, either. You go ahead and pick something, and I'll have the same."

"How about this chopped steak smothered with onions and a order of French fries or a baked potato? The bread and drink come with it."

"Sounds good. But I'll have the baked potato. Little afraid of

French food. Heard one of the men back at camp talking about the French eating snails. They didn't call them snails. Some fancy name. Think I'll take the potato. I know what they are."

The porter came back and said, "Ready to order?"

"Yes. We both want the chopped steak, a baked potato, biscuits and an orange drink --. Nehi if you have any."

He wrote their order on his note pad, smiled, and said, "Be about twenty minutes before it's ready. Would you like a drink while you are waiting?"

"Think I will," said John.

"What kind of drink? the porter asked.

"A glass of cold water. That's what you drink when you get thirsty, isn't it?"

The porter was speechless. He'd never heard this in the twenty years he had worked in the dinning cars.

"I'll have the same," Bill said.

"I'll be right back with your drinks," he said.

The porter brought their water, two glasses, and a big pitcher full of water. He didn't want to ask them any more questions about their meal.

When he set their meals on the table before them they were covered with bowl-like lids. The porter removed the lids, and on big plates were big patties of beef with heaps of steaming onions on them, big potatoes, packs of butter, and sour cream. The drink were not Nehi's, but they were bottles of orange drink along with two glasses filled with ice. The porter handed John the piece of paper he had written the order on.

"Here is your check," he said.

"What's the check for?" John asked.

"It shows how much you owe for your meals."

"We don't have any money, but we have this voucher from our Captain. He said they would buy our lunch."

John handed the two pieces of paper to the porter. He looked at them, wrote the amount that the meals cost and handed them back. "You must sign the voucher." He handed John a pen, and he signed his and gave the pen to Bill. "Thank you, Sir. I hope you enjoy your meal. If you decide that you want a desert, I'll add it to the ticket."

They finished eating their meal and decided they would have desert. John waved to the porter, and he came to their table. "What do you have for desert," John asked?

"We have several different kinds of pies and cakes and different flavors of ice cream."

"What do you recommend?"

"The French vanilla ice cream is very good."

"We don't want any French food. Do you have apple pie?"

"Sure do. And what flavor ice cream?"

"I'll have strawberry," John said.

"I like chocolate," said Bill.

"Coming up," the porter said as he walked away.

When they finished eating, they went back to the seats that they left. "Sure serve good meals on these trains," John said. "Don't know why they keep trying to sell you the French food. Probably can't get rid of it."

John and Bill both dozed off to sleep. The big meal and the clicking of the wheels on the track had put both of them in a trance. They never imagined that what was happening to them today would ever happen to a couple of poor mountain boys. It was like a dream for them.

They were wide awake when the conductor said for everyone to get their belongings together. They were nearing the station in Columbus, Georgia, home of the largest infantry training camp in the world, Fort Benning.

Fort Benning

The train was going very slow now as it entered the station. "Hope they didn't lose our duffel bags. All of our clothes and things are in them bags. Don't expect they left them on the other train in Atlanta," John said.

When the train stopped and the conductor opened the doors, John and Bill were the first to get off. They looked around to see if they could find their belongings. "Don't see them," said Bill. Better ask someone in the station."

John went to the ticket window. "Hate to bother you, but can you tell me where I can get the duffel bag that I checked in over at Fort Bragg?"

"It will be about twenty minutes before the baggage will be ready to pick up. Do you have the ticket that they gave you when you turned in your bag?"

"Sure do," John said.

"Have a seat over there, and it won't be long until you can claim your bag."

"Another thing, Sir. I need to make a telephone call. Where

are the phones?"

"Over on that wall in the booths. If it's a local call you will need a nickel. They are pay phones."

John put his hands in his pockets but couldn't find any money. "Do you have a nickel," he asked Bill?

"Got a quarter. Guess the ticket man would change it."

"I've got some money, but I keep it in a money belt that I have under my shirt. Don't want to lose it. I'm planning on sending it to my Mom in the next letter I write her. Go get the quarter changed into five nickels. May have to call more than once for someone to come and pick us up. I have the phone number wrote on the back of this envelope. We have to report to a Captain Brown."

John said to Bill, "Wonder what that noise is outside? Sounds like a wagon running on a rocky road."

He went to the window, and sure enough it was a wagon. Instead of a horse or mule pulling it, there was a man doing the pulling. It was loaded with all kinds of suit cases, and there they were, the two duffel bags.

As soon as the wagon stopped the ones who were waiting for their luggage lined up. They gave the porter their tickets, and he would get whatever they had checked in earlier when they got on the train.

John handed him his ticket, and Bill handed him his. When they had their bags, they went back into the station to make their phone call.

"You want to call?" John asked Bill.

"No. You call. It makes me nervous to talk on a phone. Never done it but a couple of times. You do the calling. Here's the nickel."

"John picked up the receiver, held it close to his ear, and dialed the number that was on the envelope. Someone said, "That will be five cents, please." He dropped the nickel in the money slot.

The phone rang on the other end. Someone picked up and said, "Company C, Captain Brown's office. Can I help you?"

"I was told to call when I got to the train station here and someone would come and get us."

"Who is calling."

"My name is John Dowdy, and Bill Wolff is with me."

"Wait just a minute."

John kept the phone to his ear, and soon someone said, "Captain Brown is expecting you two. He said for you to relax in the waiting room at the station and someone would come for you right away."

"Thank you," John said.

He put the receiver back on the hook. "May as well take it easy," he said to Bill.

About twenty minutes later, a soldier came into the waiting room and was looking around. He spotted John and Bill sitting on a long wooden bench in the center of the room.

"Are you two soldiers the ones that I am supposed to take back to camp?"

"Guess so," John said. "Are you the one that Captain Brown sent for us?"

"That's me," he replied. "All ready to go?"

"Guess so. Kind of tired. Been on a train all day."

"Get your bags and let's get going. Nearly chow time. You fellows hungry?" he asked.

"Sure are," they both answered.

"Guess Captain Brown will see you before you eat. I think you will like him. He is all business when it comes to his company and the Army. But he is a good man who takes care of his men. He doesn't have any favorites. Everyone in the outfit is his family. If you get a promotion, you can bet your life that you have earned it."

When they entered the base, there was a big sign that said, "WELCOME TO FORT BENNING – US ARMY". It didn't take long to notice the difference between this camp and Fort Bragg. Instead of sand and pine trees, everything was green, and there was grass instead of sand. As they passed the barracks they could see a difference in where the soldiers lived. Most of the buildings were brick instead of the old wooden buildings like they'd had at Bragg. Both thought they would like it here.

Captain Brown

The driver stopped in front of a big brick building. "Captain Brown's office is the second door on the right. His name is on the door. Better knock before you go in. Be sure to take off your caps."

"Thanks for giving us a ride from the train station," John said.

"Nothing to it. That's part of my job. See you guys around," he said as he drove away.

John and Bill set their bags down inside the building and went to the second door on the left. The sign on the door read, "Captain Jason Brown, Commanding officer, Company C, 3RD Infantry Division". They removed their caps, and John knocked on the door.

"Come in," someone said.

John opened the door and behind a big desk they saw their new boss. He was man who looked like he was in his fifties with graying hair and a smile on his face. He stood, and when John and Bill saluted him he returned it.

"Glad you men made the trip OK. I'll not keep you long. I'll talk with you tomorrow."

He picked up the phone and said, "Corporal Johnson, would you come to my office? He put the phone back and said, "Corporal Johnson will show you where you will be staying while here. He will also show you where the Mess Hall is, and you will learn where the other offices are located after you have been here a few days."

Johnson came into the office. "You need me, Sir?"

"Yes. Show these two men where Sergeant Henderson's barracks is. He is expecting them and has a couple of bunks ready. See you tomorrow around 10:00."

They exchanged salutes and left the office.

Johnson said, "Follow me and I'll show you where Henderson's barracks is. You are lucky to be assigned to his platoon. He has the best bunch of men in the whole company. They take first place in every contest they enter. Barracks No. 9. Here you are, your future home."

They entered the barracks and went to the Sergeant's room located at the end of the barracks. Johnson knocked on the door, and the Sergeant said, "Who's there?"

"This is Johnson from the Captain's office. I have two men here who the Captain assigned to your platoon."

"Come on in," he said. "The door isn't locked."

When Johnson opened the door he said, "This is PFC Dowdy, and this is Private Wolff."

Sergeant Henderson stood up from his chair and said, "Welcome to Charley company. My name is Henderson. Born and raised in Georgia and still here. The Captain mentioned you two the other day. Said he looked your records over and decided that you deserved the best, so he assigned you to my platoon. Glad to have you. Come on and I'll show you where your bunks are."

John and Bill unpacked their duffel bags and made their bunks.

"Let's go eat," one of the soldiers said to John. "Come on and I'll show you where the Mess Hall is."

"Thanks," John said as he was leaving the barracks.

The next morning was the same as it had been at Fort Bragg. Up at 06;00, roll call, breakfast, and fall out at 08:00 for whatever was on the schedule.

Sergeant Henderson told John and Bill that the Captain wanted to see them at his office at 09:00. "When you get back, I'll tell you what you are going to do today."

John knocked on the Captain's office door.

"Who is it?" the Captain asked.

"PFC Dowdy and Pvt Wolff."

"Come in," he said.

They exchanged salutes, and he said, "At ease. I had a call from Fort Bragg this morning and was told some bad news. Captain Pugh wanted me to tell you two. Yesterday Sergeant Davis was in an automobile accident and they have him in the Duke Hospital. Said a truck hit him head on. They think he will live but may never be able to do anything more than a desk job. I didn't want to tell you this, but your Captain insisted because of the friendship between you and Sergeant Davis. You can report back to Sergeant Henderson."

They saluted each other. John and Bill left the Captain and went back to the barracks. "Sergeant Davis should have let us ride the camp bus yesterday and this wouldn't have happened to him. Sure hope he gets well again."

The Shoot Off

They joined the rest of the platoon at the rifle range.

"I saw in your records that you are an expert rifleman," Sergeant Henderson said to John.

"I guess I can hold my own when it comes to handling a gun. Been hunting squirrels, rabbits, and everything else that we could eat since I was six or seven years old. Dad didn't believe in wasting bullets by missing whatever you shot at. They cost money, and we didn't have any to waste."

"How would you like to shoot in a contest for me?"

"OK by me. I'll give it my best. What kind of contest?"

"Well," Sergeant Hammonds in A platoon has a man who he said no one at Fort Benning could beat when it comes to shooting a rifle. And, so far, no one has beat him. I would like to shut him up with all his bragging. I'll challenge him. We will set a Saturday date so we can get a good crowd out to the firing range. Think you can beat him?"

"Never tried to beat anybody. I just like to shoot a gun. I need to shoot the rifle I have now sand get the sights set. May be a little different from my gun back at Bragg."

"We'll go to the range on Monday and you can get in a little practice. That OK with you?"

"I'll do my best," John said. "Bill is a good shot," he said to his Sergeant. "Like to have him along when we go practice."

Everything was set for the shoot off between the man from A platoon and PFC Dowdy of C platoon. It would be next Saturday right after lunch. Both of the Sergeants got the news out so there would be a good crowd to cheer for their favorite rifleman. Sergeant Henderson said the Captains of A and C platoons had been invited.

"You are kind of getting me off to a fast start," John said to Sergeant Henderson. "All you know about me is what you read in the papers sent from Fort Bragg."

"Not worried a bit," said Henderson. "Going to shut that big mouth of Hammonds.'"

All the talk that week was about the new soldier taking on the champ of Fort Benning. John went to the rifle range a couple of times and said he had a good gun. He wasn't too excited about the shoot off. He asked if Bill could be in the target pit to help raise and lower the target. He knew that having Bill watching there would be no cheating.

The big day had arrived. All who were going to the firing range crammed down their lunches. They didn't want to miss this big event. When Sergeant Henderson arrived with John and Bill there was a pretty good crowd there. Sergeant Hammonds and his sharp shooter were waiting.

The Sergeants introduced John to his competition. "This is Corporal Dotson, the best rifleman around," said Sergeant Hammonds.

"This is PFC Dowdy, the best squirrel hunter on Little Sam Mountain up in North Carolina," said Henderson.

Everybody had a good laugh.

"Are you ready to start? The rules are that there will be three rounds of shooting. Each round will be five shots. The man who wins two out of the three will be the winner. Does everyone agree?

"There will be a man from each team in the target pit. Are you ready?" Sergeant Henderson asked Hammonds.

"Ready," he said.

"You are the champion, so you will shoot first."

"Let's get started."

The Corporal fired his first five shots. The target was brought from the pit. There were five holes in the six-inch bulls-eye.

"Look at that," said Hammonds. "Perfect."

John took his place and fired five quick rounds. The target was brought from the pit. There was only one hole, and it was in dead center of the target.

The Captains had been appointed as the judges. They said, "Looks like Sergeant Henderson's man wins the first round."

The Corporal fired his second round. When the judges looked, there were only four holes, and they were all in the eye. John shot five more rounds. When they looked at the target, there was only one hole again in the center of the eye.

"Looks like PFC Dowdy is the new champion," the Captains said.

The crowd went wild with their whoops and yelling. The soldiers from A platoon were leaving. C platoon was having a great time celebrating their victory over A platoon. Sergeant Henderson and Captain Brown were all smiles.

In the following weeks and months, the training was a lot harder than the first three months. The hours were longer, and the training was different, also. Instead of using dummy hand grenades like they did at Bragg, they now used real live grenades and actually blew up targets. They also learned to crawl on their bellies under real live fire a little above them. They had to cross rivers on ropes and do many other things they might face during real battles.

It was December 7, 1941. News came over the radio that the country was at war. The Japanese had bombed Pearl Harbor. They were an ally of the Germans and Italians. The country was not prepared for a war. The Germans were about to invade and take England. The United States needed to help the English as much as they could. Great Britain was asking for help in Africa to stop the Germans from invading England next.

The War

After December the 7th , everywhere you went all the talk was about the war. All the training bases everywhere were being overrun with new soldiers to be trained. They came by buses and trains. New camps were being built. Every soldier was wondering what he would be doing and where he would be going.

Captain Brown had all of his company to meet at the base theater. It was not a movie this time. The captain didn't have a long speech and came to the reason for the meeting when everyone was there.

"Men," he began. "I don't know if I have good news or if it is bad news. I was informed yesterday that I was to get my company ready for moving. The memo said that further instructions would be given later. No one is to tell others about our moving. I want you all to get all your equipment together, packed and ready to move anytime I give the orders. This is all I know at the present. I will keep you informed as I receive future information. Your are dismissed."

"Wonder where we are going?" John said to Bill.

"Be afraid to guess," Bill said.

The next day there was a notice on the bulletin board in the barracks announcing several promotions. John was promoted to Sergeant as a squad leader. Bill was promoted to Corporal as an assistant squad leader. Sergeant Henderson was promoted to a Master Sergeant. There were other promotions to squad leader. Something big was about to happen when the orders came for the company to move.

The order came. The company would be leaving at 08:00 the next morning. The troops weren't told anything else.

They had an early breakfast, were loaded in trucks, and were taken to the train station. There was a special train waiting for them on a side track. They went from the trucks to the train and got on. Soon they were all on and the train backed from the side track to the main rail-line and were on their way. To where, none of them knew. It looked like they were traveling east. The train didn't stop for anything. They were given box-lunches to eat.

They seemed to be getting near the ocean. John said, "See all the sea birds flying out there?"

Sure enough; they were getting near the ocean. They began to see fishing boats and other small ships. The train stopped near a dock where a large ship was anchored. They unloaded from the train and marched straight onto the ship. There were already many other soldiers on the ship.

"Don't know where they came from. Guess they are the same as we are. Going somewhere but not knowing when or where?"

When they were all on the ship, they were shown where they would be sleeping -- down flights of stairs and into sections that had hammock-type beds swinging on chains from the ceiling. Not an inch of space was wasted. They were given a layout of the ship and a schedule of when and where they would eat.

"Sure hope this is a short trip," Bill said. "Kind of crowded down here."

They heard the ship's engines start and they began to move. They were on their way, but to where? It wasn't long before they were going up and down. The bunks on the chains were swinging back and forth.

"Never been on anything like this before. Makes your belly feel funny," John said.

Some of the men were already turning white and trying to vomit. "Think I'll go up and get some air," John said.

"I'll go with you," said Bill. "I'm kind of light headed and need some fresh air.

They climbed the stairs and went out on the deck. "Wow! Look at them big water waves. Looks like small mountains. No wonder we are going up and down. Wonder where we are," Bill said? "Don't see any land. Just water every way I look."

Ten days had passed, and John and Bill were up on the deck when Bill said, "Look over there, John. Looks like land."

"Sure does," John said. "Guess we are about to get to the place we are going. Must be some far-away country. Wonder if they talk the same as we do?"

"We'll soon know," Bill said. "See. The land is getting bigger."

About an hour later the ship was at a dock, and the dock hands were putting big ropes around the posts on the dock.

Somehow they kept from getting mixed up with the soldiers from the other companies that were getting off the ship. John and Bill's company was all together on the dock.

The First Sergeant said, "Fall in!" They soon were in marching formation and moving toward a train near the docks. These train cars were different from the ones back home. They were smaller and had little rooms down the side, sort of private like. John's company was the only one on this train.

Wondering again where they were headed, Bill said, "Sure will be glad to get my feet back on solid ground again."

"Me too," said John.

After a day's ride, the train pulled up to another dock where there were several ships tied up. After leaving the train, they marched to the dock and onto a smaller ship.

There were English soldiers on this ship. John asked one of them where they were going. "Don't know, Mate," he said. "I have a feeling that we are headed to North Africa. The bloody Germans are helping the Italians, and our boys need a little help."

The English soldier was right. The next day they were unloading at a port near Casablanca in Morocco, Africa.

John said to Bill, "Maybe we should have stayed at Bragg. I bet we are a thousand or more miles from North Carolina. And I am getting tired of eating the cold meals we've had since we left Fort Benning."

"Me, too," Bill said.

They were loaded on trucks and taken inland several miles from the ship dock to a "tent city". There were English soldiers stationed there and they were to be their guest for a few days. After everyone was assigned a tent, they ate their first hot meal since leaving the states. It didn't taste like what they were used to eating, but it was a lot better than the cold cuts they had been eating.

They rested for a few days and then were told that they were going to the front lines to help defeat the German soldiers who had a leader called "The Desert Fox".

John was talking with Sergeant Henderson after the meeting and asked why they called this German general The Desert Fox. "I guess it's because he outsmarts the English Army every time they think they have him cornered and thinking they will capture or kill him. He always finds a way to escape."

"Bet I could hem him up," John said. "We had the same problems with the foxes back home. They would get our chickens if they could, but we set traps for them where they didn't think they were. We 'out-foxed' them."

"You may get your chance to try catching his soldiers off guard."

There were ten men assigned to John's squad. Bill was one of them. They would go and search out the Germans. They were to capture them if possible and kill them if they fought back. John didn't want to kill another person regardless of who they were.

As they were moving forward, everything seemed quiet. This didn't last very long. They heard a machine gun firing to their left.

"Must be shooting at one of our other squads," Bill said. "Better spread out and keep your eyes open. Don't want to walk into one of the Fox's traps."

They were about ten feet apart, moving forward when a machine gun opened fire on John's squad. Someone screamed, "I'm hit! I'm hit!"

Everyone found shelter in a ditch or behind a tree. John crawled on his belly to where the soldier who was calling for help was lying. When he got there, the soldier was lying on his face. John noticed that he had quit asking for help. He put his hand on the wounded soldiers shoulder and turned him over.

When he saw the face of the soldier he said, "Oh no! It can't be." He was looking at his best friend and Army buddy. As tears began to run from his eyes he said, "Bill ... Bill." There was no answer. He put his hand on Bill's chest. There was no sign of a heartbeat. "They have killed my best friend," he said. "They will pay for this, I promise."

He took the hand grenades from Bill's belt and began crawling around the side of the hill toward where the shooting was coming from. After a few yards John was able to get up and run. He was soon behind where the machine gun was set up and firing on his men.

"They are the ones who shot Bill," he said to himself. He got as close as he could, took three grenades from his belt, and lay two on the ground. He pulled the pin and threw the first one, and before it hit the ground he had the second on its way as he grabbed the third one to throw. When the shooting stopped and the smoke cleared, there was only one German soldier standing. He was looking for a way to get away. John raised his rifle and shot once, and there was no one moving. They were all dead. John had changed from a peaceful soldier to a killing machine. Before this war was over, the enemy would pay for what had happened this day, he vowed.

The Americans and British were moving at a fast pace north and the Desert Fox and his men were retreating toward Italy. He moved all of his Army to Italy and put them under the command of an Italian General. He then went Berlin, a defeated general.

John said to Sergeant Henderson, "If the British would quit stopping twice every day to drink their cup of tea, we could end this war a lot quicker."

"They like their tea just the way we like a good cup of coffee," Henderson said. They have done the tea thing since the beginning of time and have no reason to stop now."

Winter was just around the corner when the Americans had more companies of US soldiers join them, and they left the command of the British General. From here on, they would fight as the American Army. The zones were divided so the British would go in a certain direction and the Americans another direction.

John was a seasoned soldier now and was using his skill of being a mountain boy to move through the rugged mountains of

Italy. He knew how to pick the easy way around a mountainside. For someone who never wanted to shoot another human, John had really changed. He no longer took prisoners and preferred to shoot the enemy. If they had their hands on their heads and wanted to be taken as a prisoner, he would let someone else do the taking. He would not shoot a defenseless soldier.

The war went well in Italy. All the Germans were moved to help with the fighting on the Russian front, and the German generals were expecting an invasion from the troops that were gathering in England. This left only the Italian Army to defend their country. They threw down their guns and gave up. Many of the prisoners were shipped to England to work on farms.

But this war was a long way from being over. The Germans were leaving the countries they had occupied occupying and returning to Germany and France to defend them from the expected invasion by the American and British armies that were in England.

John was bitter toward the Germans because of what they did to his best friend in Africa. John would never see him again. He said to himself, "I will never feel sorry for any foreign soldier. I'll only take them as a prisoner when they have no gun and have their hands on their head. If they have any type of a weapon I think they could use to kill one of our soldiers, I will kill them."

This was not the John Dowdy who had lived on Little Sam Mountain. This was the infantry soldier, Sergeant John Dowdy, US Army. And from the day that Bill was killed, John did what he promised: He was getting revenge.

Charles C. Fletcher

Dinner With Tony

John had become friends with the soldier who replaced Bill after he was killed. He was from somewhere in New York City. John never knew his last name, only his first: Tony. His family had come to America many years ago from Italy. Tony could speak Italian and was a great help to John.

Tony said to John, "Sergeant, why don't you and I go scouting for a good Italian restaurant? You've never eaten any good food until you have had a real spaghetti meal, one with all the trimmings. What do you say?"

John's favorite food was a good old Canton, North Carolina, hot dog, but he was always ready to try something new.

"Let's go," he said to Tony. It's better than sitting around waiting for orders from the General.

As they went looking around, Tony was talked to the local people that they met. John didn't understand a single thing that they were talking about. If they spoke to him, he just shook his head for "yes" or "no". Sometimes Tony would laugh because of John's answer and tell him what he said by shaking his head for an answer. This didn't bother him at all.

They soon found what the local people called the best eating place in town, and maybe the best in Italy. "We'll try this one," Tony said.

A waiter met them at the door. Tony said something to him, and he gave them a bow and motioned for them to follow him. He seated John and Tony at a table, gave each a large folder with all the things that they had that they could order. John took a look at it and shook his head.

"Be afraid to pick one of these. Could be like the snails that they eat in France. I may get hungry," he said, "but I will never get hungry enough to eat snails. They look nasty. You pick out something," he said to Tony. "You can read that kind of writing. I can't. Don't think I will ever talk and write like all the people we have met in the Army. I'll stick with the way we talk on Little Sam Mountain.

"This looks awful good," Tony said. "Spaghetti with sauce, meat balls, real Italian bread, a fresh green salad, and a bottle of the best house wine. What do you say, Sergeant?"

"Sounds good to me. You do the ordering. They can't understand a single thing I say, and I don't know what to say either. Tony, you give the waiter our order."

"OK," Tony said as he motioned to the waiter.

It sounded like a bunch of guinea fowls at sundown the way they were talking and waving their hands. The waiter left and Tony said, "Everything is taken care of, and you will soon be eating like you have never eaten before. The Italians know how to fix a good meal."

It wasn't long until two young girls came to their table and began to set covered bowls of food on the table. One of the girls, who looked like she was somewhere around sixteen years old, kept looking at John and smiling. Tony said something to her and she blushed.

"Mossell thinks you are very cute," he said to John.

"Who is Mossell?" John asked.

"The little girl with the long black hair."

"Tell her I think she is a pretty girl. She sort of looks like Sarah, the girl back on Little Sam Mountain that I may marry when I go back home. We are sort of engaged to each other. This means that I won't have another girl friend. Well, not one I would be in love with."

The girls left and soon returned with more food. They removed the covers from the bowls and began to put the food on big plates setting before each man. First, there was a mountain of spaghetti. Then a sauce that looked like tomato juice was poured over the spaghetti. They began to lay little round balls of meat on top of all this. The one that had her eye on John was serving him and the other girl was fixing Tony's food. They uncovered a big tray of bread that was sliced sort of sideways instead of across like John's mom sliced it. After a large bottle of wine was set on the table, the girls left.

John and Tony picked up their forks and began to eat. Tony was going great but John couldn't get any food to stay on his fork. Tony noticed that John was having a hard time, so he said to him, "John, watch how I stick the fork in the spaghetti and twist it. This rolls it up into a ball so it will stay on the fork."

It didn't take John long to get the hang of eating spaghetti. He put one of the little balls of meat in his mouth and began to chew. He wasn't making much headway with chewing it up. He said to Tony, "This meat is a little tough. Must have come from an old skinny cow."

They noticed that the waiter was standing behind them. Tony said something to the waiter. He answered Tony, and Tony said to John, "The meat balls didn't come from cow meat. They were made from horse meat.

John opened his mouth and let the ball of meat fall out of his mouth and on the floor where it bounced a couple of times. He took his napkin and wiped his mouth.

"I'm not eating any horse meat. I'll have the spaghetti and bread. You can have all the meat balls," he said to Tony.

"How about a glass of wine to wash the food down?" Tony said to John.

"Never have tasted any kind of drink with alcohol in it. Our family had a bad experience from seeing Dad drinking some moonshine one time. All of us children made a promise to our Mom that we would never touch the stuff." He continued to tell Tony the full story about his Dad and Ledbetter's moonshine.

After John was finished telling his story, Tony took a little sip from his glass of wine and set it aside. He never touched it again.

They finished their dinner and were discussing where they may be heading next. "Never can tell," said John. There are rumors about going into France. This could be the easiest way to attack the Germans on the ground."

Their talk was interrupted. The two girls who brought the food were back at the table. The older girl began talking to Tony. The other one was looking at John and smiling.

"Sure wish this pretty little girl would quit looking at me the way she does. It makes me nervous and makes me think of Sarah. Sarah is my girlfriend back home on Little Sam Mountain. Sure would like to see her. Bet she is as lonely as I am, me being all this far from home."

"We'd better get back to the outfit. Can't never tell when orders will come down for us to move out," Tony said.

"Guess we'd better," John said. "The top brass never tells us anything until the last minute. Don't want them to move and leave me behind. Probably never find them in this country. You pay for the dinner, and I will give you my part when we get back to the house we are staying in. I have my money in the money belt under my shirt. Don't want to show my belly in front of these girls."

Tony paid the waiter, and they left the restaurant. As they were walking along the street, small children followed them, pulling their arms and asking for chewing gum and candy.

"Chewing gum, Yank. Chocolate, Yank," they were saying. Some even asked for cigarettes. These were probably the only English words they knew.

John and Tony had to tell them no because they didn't have anything to give them. These children were poor and hungry. "They remind me of children from a few families who live in the mountains back in North Carolina," John said.

John and all the other men in his company didn't do any-thing but hang around for another week. John wanted to write letters home and to Sarah, but he didn't have any way of getting them in the mail that would be sent back to the States.

The days of rest were short. Word came to get everything packed and be ready to move on the next day. Neither John nor any of the other soldiers were told where they would be going. Only the top officers knew. The soldiers would be told after they were on their way. This was the Army's way of doing things.

The next morning the soldiers were given a day's supply of "K" rations for their meals. They loaded all of their equipment onto trucks, and they also rode in "6X6" trucks.

The officers led the way, and all the trucks followed. After about four hours, the convoy stopped. All the men got out of the trucks to stretch a little and were told to eat their lunch before moving on. They still didn't know where they were going.

Just before dark they knew that they were near the ocean.

There were seagulls and other birds flying about that were found near the sea. The convey stopped, and everyone in the company was told to assemble in a field nearby. The commanding officer of the company stood in the back of his jeep and said, "Men, I hate to tell you this, but we are going to take another boat ride. You all know that the Normandy invasion is making progress from Utah and Omaha beaches. We have been ordered to help cut off the German Army in the south of France. Where and when we will land is a top secret. My order to you is to be ready for combat from the moment you get on the ship. Eat and rest for about thirty minutes and then load up for the ride to the docks. Good luck, and may God watch over you."

They now knew that they were going to France. When they got to the docks where the ships were tied up, John knew that this was a big operation. There were thousands of military persons every way he looked. They were not all American soldiers. He saw English, French, Canadian, and one company of New Zealand soldiers.

John heard a noise that sounded a little like someone was trying to make music. He looked up the dock a ways, and here came what looked like a platoon of soldiers, but they were not in uniform. They all had dress-like skirts on like women wear but a lot shorter. They had on tam-like hats and socks that came above their knees. They were following someone squeezing and blowing into a big bag. This was where the weird music was coming from.

"What in the world is that?" John asked a soldier standing next to him.

"Those are soldiers from Scotland. I hear that they are real good at fighting," he said.

"How could they slip upon the enemy with all that noise? And I bet their legs and other parts get cold. Makes me freeze just looking at them wearing them short dresses."

After all of the company that John belonged to was on the ship, he managed to get his ten-man patrol together. When the fighting began his men knew what to do as a team.

The ships were all loaded and began to leave the docks. They were moving in the same direction, but there was some kind of a pattern in their leaving. After they were away from shore a ways, there came an announcement over the ships speakers:

"The code name for this operation is 'Dragoon'. Today is August 15, 1944. We will be going ashore at a little French town by the name of "Saint Tropez". We will establish a beachhead and begin our movement across France to join the troops that landed at the Normandy beaches. This will cut off the supplies to all the German troops that are in the lower part of France. You all know what your job is, but I must warn you that there are a lot of temptations to take your mind off of the war. Don't let these things, like all the pretty girls, lead you astray. If you wander off, you will be court marshaled. You are all seasoned soldiers and know what you are here for. The future of the world is at stake, and it is up to you and me to make it a safer world. Good luck, and may God protect you."

"I hope this is the last foreign country we go to," John said. I'll sure be glad when we get back to the good old USA. Sure wish the Army would put a hotdog in these "K" rations instead of spam or stew. Bet I could eat a dozen if I was back in Canton.

"Look," John said. "There it is, Southern France. The Navy ships are firing their big guns at the enemy on the beaches. It won't be long before we will be going ashore."

John got his squad together and began checking to see if they had all of their ammunition and were ready to meet the enemy.

Wounded

The ship that John and his company was on headed toward the beach where they were to land. They stopped moving, and rope ladders were thrown over the side of the ship. The soldiers closest to the side began to climb down to smaller landing craft. As soon as one left for the beach another took its place alongside the ship. Soon John and his men were making their way down the side of the ship.

"Don't get separated," John hollered to his men. "Got to stay together," he said.

The small landing craft that John and his squad was on headed toward the beach at full speed. It soon stopped moving, the front opened, and everyone headed toward shore. They waded in cold water that was up to their arms. They had their rifles above their heads to keep them from getting wet.

When they were out of the water and on the beach, all of John's squad were soon together. They were surprised that they were not under fire from the enemy. Shelling from the ships had them retreating to get out of range of the shelling. It was great that no one was getting killed from this landing.

As they moved across France to join the soldiers who were fighting their way inland from the invasion at Normandy, they meet with very little resistance. Only a few snipers who had become separated from their outfits and were hid out in the farm houses across the country side fired at them.

John's company led the way as they marched toward St Low. There they joined General Patton's Third Army. He would be their commander for the rest of the war.

Now the fighting wasn't easy anymore. The Germans didn't want to give up the city of St Low. The Germans who didn't retreat, finally surrendered and John and his squad continued north.

As John and all the others in Patton's Army moved toward the German border, there was another enemy they would soon be facing: the weather. It was something that the American forces were not prepared for. Not only was it a different kind of cold weather, but was also very wet and muddy. The Germans had an advantage over their enemy. They were accustomed to this kind of weather.

When John's company was near a small French town called Bar-Le-Duc, and he and his squad were on a night patrol, out of nowhere a machine gun began firing at them.

"Take cover!" John hollered.

It was too late for some of them. Several were hit by the bullets from the machine gun. The men of the squad then became separated.

John moved around trying to get the squad back together. All of a sudden, John heard a burst from a machine gun from another direction. His legs felt like he had been stung by a bunch of yellow jackets, a kind of bee that was common back in the mountains where John grew up. The stinging soon turned to pain.

"I've been hit!" John hollered. The pain was so great that

John soon lost consciousness.

It was day light when John woke up. He looked around and saw that he was in a big tent. As he looked around he saw rows of cots. There were people in some of them, and some were empty. All the people moving around were dressed in white.

"Where am I?" John asked a man with a mask on his face.

"You are in a field hospital," he said to John. "A patrol found you this morning in the snow. You were one of the lucky ones. They brought two others in who were still alive. All the others they located were dead. You had a lot of lead in your legs. I'm a doctor. I removed all the metal I could find, but there may be other pieces. You were frozen and have some frostbite. We're moving you back from the front, and you'll probably end up in England at a hospital where they can do more for you than we can here. We only try to keep the wounded alive until they can be moved to regular hospital. Good luck, Sergeant. Hope everything goes well and you will be back in the frontlines soon."

"This can't be," John thought. "It's only a bad dream."

The next morning John was put on a stretcher and loaded into an ambulance.

"Going for a ride," the ambulance driver said to John.

"Where are we going? John asked?

"Not too far," the driver answered. "Somewhere around twenty miles. I've made this trip lots of times but never checked how far it was. Don't make a difference to me," he said". "Not going anywhere until this war is over. Sure is a sad job that I have, seeing you poor boys all shot up. I don't like this job, but someone has to do it. At least there is a bright side for me. I feel like I'm helping you to get well again, But it's still a sad job."

As the ambulance came to a stop and the back door was opened, John saw several large air planes sitting side by side. Two soldiers unfastened the stretcher that John was on, pulled it out of the ambulance, and carried him to one of the planes. When he was inside the plane, he saw soldiers on stretchers everywhere he looked. He was about to take his first airplane ride.

The door was closed, John heard the roar of engines, and he felt the plane beginning to move. As the roar became louder, the plane moved faster over a bumpy-like road. Soon the bumps were gone, and everything was smooth. Even the roar was less.

Everything was smooth for about an hour, and then the bumps were back. "We are on the ground again," John said to himself.

When the plane stopped and the door was opened, John could see a row of Army ambulances. They were there to take him and all the other wounded soldiers to a hospital.

John didn't notice the pain from his wounds. He was thinking about where he was going and what was ahead for him. He was thinking about his family back home on Little Sam Mountain, wondering if he would be seeing them again. He also was thinking about Sarah Smith, wondering if she had received the last letter he had written to her.

"Ready to go, Buddy?" someone asked.

"Where are we going, John asked?"

"Taking you to the hospital at Malvern. Just a wide place in the road, but there is a pretty good sized town nearby called Worcester. Pretty good place to go when you can find time off from duty. Got a lot of good Pubs, a movie house, a hotel that is run by the USO, and the best part is that there are lots and lots of pretty English girls. All the young English men are off fighting in the war. Only the girls and the ones that are too old to be in the service are left on the home front. Better get you to the hospital so they can get started fixing whatever is wrong with you. Soon as you are able, go to town for the weekend. Do you good to get away from the Army for a few hours."

Hospital

John was soon in a real bed with clean white sheets. Nurses all dressed in white with cute little caps on their heads were all about.

"Don't know what good that cap does," John thought. "Don't cover their head. Just sticks up in front of their hair."

He had just gotten comfortable when a doctor came to his bed. "My name is Doctor Clark. I need to take a look at your wounds."

He moved the cover off of John and pulled up the hospital gown that he was wearing.

"Don't look too bad, but there is a lot of swelling, and it looks like there is more metal in you. I'll arrange for surgery. Probably first thing tomorrow. Having much pain?" he asked John.

"Not too bad," John answered. "Kind of getting used to it, I guess."

Doctor Clark pulled the sheet back over John and said, "I'll see you tomorrow morning."

The orderly didn't bring John anything to eat the next morning. "Don't I get any breakfast?" John asked.

"No Sir," the orderly said. "Doctor's orders. You will soon be going for surgery. They will put you to sleep so you won't feel any pain while they cut on you. The ether that they use to put you to sleep sometimes makes you really sick if you have eaten anything for several hours before they give it to you."

"Wish I hadn't of asked you about the breakfast. You have me scared to death, all that talking about cutting, making me go to sleep, and stuff. I'm not hungry after listing to you." John turned his face away from the orderly and pulled the sheet over his head.

John was starting to doze off to sleep when someone pulled the sheet off his head. When he looked up, there stood a pretty young nurse. She smiled and said, "Ready for your breakfast, good looking?"

John looked around and didn't see anyone except the nurse. "I'm going to give you a little something so you will be relaxed when they come to take you to the operating room."

John saw that she had a needle in her hand. "Don't like to be stuck with needles, but if I must, go ahead and get it over with."

He raised his arm, the nurse pushed the pajama sleeve up, and then turned John's arm loose. "Go ahead and get it over with," he said.

"All done. Didn't you feel me stick you?"

"No. Didn't feel anything."

"Bye. See you later. Good luck."

John watched her as she was walking to another patient. "Pretty girl," he was thinking. "Sarah would get mad if she knew I was looking at another girl."

Soon John was asleep. The shot that he was given was working.

It wasn't long until someone said, "Ready to take a ride sol-dier?" He looked up and saw two men in long gowns with tight skull caps on their heads. "Dr Clark is ready to get you back in shape for combat. You will be as good as new when he finishes with you. Best Doctor in the Army. Sure knows what he is doing when it comes to surgery."

They lifted John out of the bed and laid him on a gurney. A strap was placed around his legs and chest to keep him from falling off.

"Hang on, Feller. We're on our way."

When John awoke, he raised his head and looked all around the room. He was confused about where he was. He saw a young Army nurse sitting beside his bed.

"That you Sarah?" he asked.

"No. I'm not Sarah. My name is June. June Henson. Who is this Sarah you were asking about when you were waking up? You called her name several times when you were in the operating room."

John began to settle down and was pretty well on his way to knowing where he was. "Sarah is the girl I am going to marry when I get back home," John said. She lives on Little Sam Mountain about a mile from where I live."

"Where is this place you call Little Sam? June asked

"It's one of the many mountains in western North Carolina. Every mountain has a different name. Usually named after the man that owns it. They call the next mountain over from Little Sam 'Big Sam' Mountain. Don't know why. Little Sam is a bigger mountain than Big Sam. Must have been two men named Sam and one was bigger than the other."

"Where are you from?" John asked June.

"I'm from a little town in the Piedmont area of North Carolina. Ever hear of Kings Mountain?" she asked.

"Heard the name somewhere. May have read about it in one of Mom's books. Didn't they have a big battle there one time?"

"Sure did," June said. "It's not too far from where you live in Canton. About seventy miles. I've met several other soldiers from there. All the boys in them mountains must be in the Army. Looks like you are awake now. I'd better take a look at some of the other patients. If you have any pain, give me a call. They will be bringing you something to eat soon. You hungry?", she asked.

"Sure am," John said. "Wouldn't have any hotdogs around here, would you?"

" Are you kidding? June said. "I've not had one since I left North Carolina. Don't guess the rest of the world knows about them, but in case you do find any, you be sure and let me know where they are. You make me hungry just talking about them. See you around," June said as she left.

A few days passed and John was up and walking the aisle of the hospital ward he was in. He had seen June several times, but the only said hello as they passed each other. "I think I'll ask if I can go outside for a walk," John said to himself.

He didn't waste any time asking. Here came nurse June down the aisle toward John.

"Could I ask you something?" John said.

"Sure you can," she said. "What do you want?"

"Would it be OK if I went outside and looked around? I would like to see where I'm at."

"I'll ask the Doctor and let you know on my next round. Be about an hour."

An hour passed, and John was waiting for his nurse to come to his ward. She came back right on time.

"What did the Doc say?" John asked before June had a chance to speak.

"He said it was OK when the weather was good and it wasn't raining. Rains a lot here in England. Seems like every other day we have rain or snow," June said. "When you go outside, you must tell the Head Nurse where you are going. Her office is at the end of the ward. There are benches under the big tree outside. This is where most of the patients sit when they go outside. You be careful and don't bump your wounds. You are about well."

"Thanks for asking the Doctor for permission," he said to June. "I'll do you a favor sometime. Buy you a hotdog if I ever find one over here."

After finishing eating his lunch, John looked outside, and it was a bright sunny day. "Think I'll look around outside," he said to himself.

He went to the nurses' station at the end of the ward. "I would like to speak to the Head Nurse," he said to the nurse sitting behind the desk.

"That's me Honey," she answered. "Can I help you?"

"I was thinking of taking a walk outside, if it's OK with you. Sort of curious as to where I'm at."

"Sort of take it easy out there, and don't wander off too far from the ward," she said to John.

John went back to his bed and got his robe. "Better wear this," he said. "May be a little chilly outside."

John walked toward the benches under the trees outside the hospital. He noticed a soldier sitting on one of the benches. He, too, had a hospital robe on, but John noticed that one of the sleeves was hanging down with no arm in it.

John walked over to where the soldier was sitting and said, "Mind if I sit with you?"

"Be glad to have you," he said. "Kind of lonesome sitting alone."

He turned his head to see who he was talking to. They were both speechless.

"Sergeant Dowdy?" he said.

"Tony?" John said. "Never expected to see any of our squad again," John said. "What happened to your arm?" John asked.

"Never expected to see you again, Sergeant. Thought that machine gun had killed all of us," Tony said.

"Tell me what happened to your arm," John said.

"I remember the shooting and you hollering for everyone to hit the ground. That was the last thing I remembered until I was awake in a tent with a doctor and several other people standing over me. I noticed that one of my arms was missing. I asked the Doctor, 'What happened to my arm?'

"The doctor began, 'When one of the squads found you, your arm was frozen to the ground. It was torn up pretty bad. Had bled a lot. I had to remove your arm to save your life. You are lucky to still be alive,' the doctor said. They sent me here for more treatments," Tony said.

"What are you doing here?" Tony asked John.

"What you told me about them finding you is what they told me," John said. "My legs and back were full of bullets from that machine gun. We must have been the only two that were still alive when they found us," John said.

John and Tony talked about what they remembered and how they could have avoided the trap they walked into that cold night in France. They didn't notice that they had company. One of the orderlies from the hospital was standing behind John and Tony.

"Time to go in," he said. "You two have been out here a long time. Don't want you to catch a cold. Enough wrong with you already. Better get back inside."

"See you again tomorrow if they will let us out," John said to Tony.

John and Tony met under the tree about everyday when the weather was good enough to be outside.

"Tony," John said, "why don't we get a pass and go to town? Do us good to get away from here for a little while. How about an overnight pass for this coming Saturday? I hear that the USO has a hotel where we can spend the night. May find a café that has some Italian food."

"That would be great," Tony said. "I'll ask as soon as we go back inside. You do the same."

Fish And Chips

John and Tony got their passes, and arrangements were made for someone to take them to town. They were not in shape to walk the five miles to town. The jeep that took them to town stopped in front of the USO hotel.

"I'll pick you two up on Sunday at about 16:00," the driver said.

As soon as John and Tony had their reservations made for a place to sleep at the hotel, they went out looking over the town of Worcester. After looking around for over an hour, they finally decided on a place where they would eat . It wasn't easy to find an eating place. There were more pubs than restaurants.

They entered the restaurant and were greeted by an older man dressed in a black suit, a white shirt, and black bow tie.

"Welcome to the Lion's Den," he said. "Is there a certain table you would like to be at?" he asked.

"Over by the window will be fine," John said. "Never been here before, so it doesn't make any difference where we sit."

"Right this way," the waiter said. He walked ahead of John

and Tony with menus in his hand.

Before John and Tony had a chance to look at the menus, not one, but two pretty girls sat at their table. The younger-looking one chose John as her customer, and the other one stood by Tony's side.

"My name is Jane, and this is Pam," said the one standing beside Tony. "Have you decided what you would like for lunch?"

"Haven't looked at the menu yet. Do you have any spaghetti and meat balls?" Tony asked.

"I've heard of that, but I've never seen or eaten any of it," June said. "I don't think our cooks would know how to prepare it."

Then Pam spoke up, "And you, Sir. What would you like?"

"Bet you don't have a hotdog," John said.

Both of the girls looked at each other then at John.

"You must be joshing," Pam said to John. "You wouldn't eat a dog, would you? I have heard that the people in the Far East sometimes eat cats and dogs, but I never heard that you Americans eat dogs."

"I wouldn't eat a dog either," John said to Pam. A hotdog is not a dog. That's just it's name. It's a weenie that has been cooked, placed in a bread bun, and has a lot of onions and chili over it. Now do you understand?"

"What is a 'weenie'?" Pam asked John. "I know what a bun and onions are, but I never saw a weenie or chili."

"A weenie is... You know .... Well at the hospital we sometimes have something like a weenie, but it is called a sausage. Well, a weenie is like what you call sausage only it has meat in it instead of sausage. And chili is ground meat with a lot of hot spices in it. Now do you get the picture?" John asked the two girls.

The girls looked at each other, and Pam said, "I think I understand what you are trying to tell me, and I now know that you wouldn't eat a poor dog."

"What do you have to eat that you think we would like?" John asked.

"Well …," Pam began. "You do know there is a war going on, and food is very scarce. We have several meals that are made from sausage with vegetables. Our soup is very good, but I think you would like an old English favorite, that being our 'fish and chips.'"

"If you say it's good, I'll have the fish and chips," John said.

Tony said he would have the same thing.

The girls left to turn in the orders for the fish and chips and returned.

"Would you like tea with your meal?" Pam asked.

"That would be fine," John said.

"You look sort of like Sarah," John said to Pam.

"Who is Sarah," Pam asked.

"Sarah is a girl back home on Little Sam Mountain. We are sort of engaged to get married when I get back home. She is about sixteen by now. How old are you, Pam? John asked.

"I am seventeen. I am the youngest child in my family. Why do you ask?" Pam said.

"Just did. Don't know why. If I wasn't promised to Sarah, I might be interested in thinking about you for my wife."

Pam blushed and said, "I'll go get your tea."

The fish and chip s were set before the two soldiers. After looking at their dinners a few moments, John said to Tony, "The fish looks like fish, but the chips look like plain old French fries. What do you think?"

"That's what they look like to me," he said.

After they had finished eating the girls came back to the table . "How was the meal?" Jane asked.

"The fish and French fries were really good, but the tea was awful warm and sweet. Needed a little ice and lemon. Not too bad," John said.

The girls went back to the kitchen. John and Tony paid for their meals and left a good tip for the girls.

"Better hurry and look around some more. Be dark pretty soon, and you can't have lights after dark. That is what the German planes look for to drop their bombs on."

They spent the night at the USO hotel, and the driver was there at 16:00 sharp to take them back to the hospital. They were tired and ready to get back in their beds. They had enjoyed their trip to town, the girls, and the fish and chips.

End Of The War

June, John's nurse, came his bed and said, "Got good news for you. The doctor said that you were well enough to go back to your outfit in France. Going to miss having you around. You sure have been a good patient. Hope to see you again sometime, but not in a hospital. If I ever pass through Canton, I'll look you and Sarah up and visit."

John didn't get much sleep that night. He was thinking about his buddies that he left when he came to the hospital, wondering how many were still in his old outfit.

A full week passed, and John had not heard any more mention of him being sent back to active duty. The suspense was getting to him. "I wish they would tell me something," he said to himself.

Spring had arrived while John was in the hospital. Most days were bright with a lot of warm sunshine. He and Tony were often found on the benches outside visiting and talking about their plans after leaving the Army. They were dreaming and planning but never gave any thought to the fact that dreams do not always come true.

It was on a Saturday morning a little after 08:00 when someone came running into John's ward. He was yelling at the top of his voice, "The War is over! The War is over! The Germans have surrendered!"

All the patients who were able to get out of bed were hugging each other and dancing all over the building. "We are going home! We are going home!" they were all hollering.

This changed the plans for sending John back to the battlefields. His services were not needed now that all the shooting had stopped. He was glad. He had seen enough of his buddies getting killed and wounded. He was ready to go home.

Going Home

Plans were made to send all the wounded soldiers back to hospitals in the States. Although John was well and didn't need any more treatments for his wounds, he was included on the list of men who were to board the hospital ship for the trip back to the USA. Waiting for orders to be shipped back to the USA seemed take months although it was only a couple of weeks.

John and Tony were together most everyday, and the thing they talked about most was what they would be doing after they were discharged from the Army. Tony talked about how he would have to adjust to doing things with his one arm. John was sort of caught up in talking about all the things that he and Sarah would be doing after they were married.

John said that they would take a few days off for a short honeymoon in Asheville. Then there was the cleaning the field of briars and bushes to make way for building their first house. After this the list of things to do was so long that John didn't want to talk about it. "I'll take care of everything as it comes up," he said.

Finally the big day arrived. Everyone was getting in an

ambulance or a truck. What they rode in depended on each one's condition.

John rode in a truck, but he had no idea where his friend Tony was. "Hope we can get together on the ship," John said to himself. "Going to be awful crowded. Must be at least three thousand patients leaving this hospital. Maybe others from some other hospital, too."

The convoy of trucks and ambulances left the hospital at Malvern and was on its way to the port where the hospital ship was waiting for them. John had managed to get a seat at the back of the truck and was enjoying the many things that he was seeing as they went through the English villages and towns. He saw houses with roofs that were covered with thatch. Then there were others that had red tile roofs. Then there were pubs as you entered a town or village. They all were named after some animal or their location: "Half Way House", "Lion's Den", "Boars Head", and so on. Never were any two names alike.

After a good four hour's drive, John began to notice sea gulls flying around. "Must be getting close to the ocean," John said to the soldier sitting beside him. "Won't be long, now".

Sure enough, the convoy was on the dock and John saw a large white ship with red crosses on its sides and the flags that were flying over the ship.

"Sure is a large ship," John said as he was getting out of the truck.

The soldiers who were in the ambulances were taken aboard the ship first and then John and all the others who could walk were marched up the gang plank. As they came aboard the ship a number was assigned to each one and a check mark placed by their names. The numbers were called out, and they were told where they would be sleeping during the trip back home. John was assigned to the number two deck. He was given a sheet of paper that had a map of the ship's layout on it and a list of the times he was to go to the dining room for his meals.

"They sure don't miss anything," John said to the soldier in the bunk next to him.

"Sure don't," his new neighbor said.

"Everyone must be on board the ship. It's beginning to move backwards from the dock," John said. "We are on our way. Wonder how long it will take to cross the ocean?

"Don't know exactly, but I heard someone say it would be ten or twelve days, depending on the weather.

"Took about that much time when I came over about three or so years ago," John said.

Nine days later the ship was met by a tug boat to move it up the river to the docks in New York City. The trip across the Atlantic Ocean had been a smooth one. There were none of the storms or high waves that were usually on the Atlantic Ocean.

All who could walk marched to a waiting train. No one knew where he was going, and no one cared as long as it was closer to home. Most all of them had been away for over three years. They were ready to get back to where it was peaceful and quite and no one was shooting at them.

Soon the train started to move slowly away from the docks. "Wonder where we are going," John asked the soldier sitting beside him.

"Heard someone on the dock watching us unload say that a lot of troops who needed more treatment at a hospital were going to Fort Dix," the soldier said. There is a large Army hospital there."

He was right. The train had slowed down and was parking on a side track near the train station. The sign on the wall read, 'Trenton, New Jersey'. This was the first of several stops for John before he would be back home again. At the station there were trucks and ambulances waiting to take them to the barracks and the hospital at Fort Dix.

John was at Fort Dix for only two days when he was given his orders and a train ticket to Fort Bragg, North Carolina. This would be his second trip to Fort Bragg, but this time he was going there to get out of the Army instead of getting into the Army. This Army base had been changed from a training center to a separation center for processing and discharging soldiers who were returning from overseas and were going home.

"This is great," John said to the officer who gave him his orders. "I'll get to visit with my old sergeant who I took Basic Training with. He was the best sergeant at Fort Bragg. May see the Captain, also. He loved his drinks but was a good company commander."

John arrived at Fort Brag, was assigned a bunk in one of the barracks, and was given a piece of paper with a schedule for what he was to do. He was going to be very busy for a couple of days.

After getting settled in his barracks, he headed toward the Captain's office. When he entered the office he noticed that the Corporal was not the one who was there when he last visited the Captain.

"I am looking for Sergeant Davis," John said to the clerk. "I think his given name is 'Brad'... 'Sergeant Brad Davis.'"

"I know Sergeant Davis. He works in the next building, but he has gone on furlough and won't be back for two weeks. Could I help you with something?" the corporal asked.

"Guess not," John said. "Just wanted to visit with him. I may not be here when he comes back," John said. "Would you tell him that Sergeant Dowdy, John Dowdy, came by to see him?"

"Sure will. Bet he will be disappointed to have missed you. When did you know him?" the corporal asked

"He was my Sergeant when I took Basic Training here over three years ago," John said. "Is the same Captain here?" John asked.

"No, my captain has been here for only about six months," he said. "There have been several Company Commanders over the last three years. Sergeant Davis was telling me about his old boss. Said he went to the Pacific with an artillery outfit and was wounded pretty bad on an invasion of some island. He never heard if he ever recovered from his wounds."

"Thanks for the information," John said.

The next day John started the process of being discharged from the Army. Everything was about the same as took place when he went into the Army. He had a complete physical, shots for all the diseases that he could have in the future, and all the other things that were required before he became a civilian again. They did leave off the GI haircut. Probably didn't think of it.

On the second day, John was informed that everything was in order and he would be leaving at 08:00 the next morning. He was given an envelope that contained his discharge papers, a bus ticket back to Canton, North Carolina, and money for two meals. There were also other instructions concerning the benefits he was to receive.

The next morning John was up early, eat breakfast, packed his duffel bag, and went to where he was to board an Army bus to take him to the bus station in town. He and others were on the bus at exactly 08:00 and on their way home.

John had ridden this route on the bus before and as interested in the scenery as he was on the last bus ride. He closed his eyes and began to think and plan the things that had to be done once he arrived home. He dozed off into a light sleep. His dreams were about Sarah and the place on Little Sam Mountain where he would build the house after he and Sarah were married.

He was awakened by the bus driver announcing, "Charlotte! Everyone gets off here."

John got off the bus and went to the bus that would be going to Asheville. "When will we be leaving?" John asked the driver standing at the bus door.

"We will be leaving in thirty minutes," he said. "You have time to eat if you want to. The food is pretty good at the snack bar in the station," the bus driver said.

John went inside and found him a seat on a stool at the counter. As soon as he sat down, a waiter asked him what he would like to eat. John was thinking of asking about a hotdog but decided to wait until he got to Canton and the Greek café.

"What do you recommend? John asked.

"The cheeseburger with French fries is very good."

"I'll have that and an orange drink," John said.

"Coming right up," the waiter said.

Before John could blink his eyes, the waiter placed a big platter before him. On one end was a big sandwich, the cheeseburger, and on the other end a big pile of potatoes. The orange drink was in a bottle.

"Need anything else, just give me a call," the waiter said.

"Could use some ketchup," John said.

As he ate, John thought back to the café in Worcester, England, and the fish and chips. The fried potatoes that he was eating were the same as the chips.

On the bus bound for Asheville, John thought, "Only twenty miles to Canton after I get to Asheville." He got comfortable, dozed off again, and returned to dreamland. All the many stops at the towns between Charlotte and Asheville didn't wake John up.

"Asheville!" the driver hollered. "Everyone will change buses here. Be sure not to leave any of your belongings on the bus.

"I'm nearly home," John said to himself. No more bus changing once I reach Canton.

It was late in the day when the bus pulled into the station at

Canton. John got off and waited for the driver to get his duffel bag from the storage compartment under the bus. He then had to find out where his family lived. He had the house address, but didn't know where the location was.

John said, "I know what I'll do. I'll go up the street to the Greek café and ask the cook where West Main Street is. He would know because he lives in town."

As he entered the café, the cook said, "Well, well, well. It's the soldier who likes my hotdogs. Welcome home, Soldier. Good to see you again. What would you like to eat? It's on the house. Ain't gonna cost you a dime."

"I didn't stop to eat, but now that I'm here, I think I'll have a couple of hotdogs and a Nehi orange drink. Sure missed them while I was gone. Couldn't find a hotdog all over the world."

When the cook brought the hotdogs John said, "I need to ask you where North Main Street is. I'm looking for 1520 North Main Street. Do you know where it is?" John asked.

"Sure do," the cook said. "When you leave, turn right, and go up one street. Turn left, go across the railroad tracks, and when you get to the stoplight, turn left again. The next street, turn left. That is North Main. The house numbers are on the front of each house. Think you can find it?" he asked.

John wiped the ketchup from his mouth with a napkin and said, "I think so. When I finish this other hotdog, we'll go over it again."

John picked up his duffel bag and left the café. All that he had to do was find 1520 North Main Street, and he would be home again.

John didn't have any trouble locating the house where his family were living. When he first saw the house at 1520 North Main, he stopped and gave it a good look.

"Sure is a big house," John said. "Must have five or six rooms.

And there is grass in the yard. Sure is a pretty place."

He walked to the porch that ran the length of the house. He set his duffel bag down and knocked on the door. John's Mom opened the door, saw John and screamed as loud as she could.

"John! John! You've come home!"

She gave him a big hug and said, "Come on in. Your dad will be home from the paper mill soon. The girls get out of school at three o'clock, and your brother gets off from work at five. You won't know the girls. They are big girls now. They will be happy to see you. They talked about their brother who was off fighting in the war all the time when they found someone who would listen to their bragging."

John was in the kitchen watching his mother cook supper and waiting for his dad to get home. He was real proud that his mom didn't have to go to the spring for water or to the wood shed for wood to heat the stove. She had a modern kitchen. A big sink that had hot and cold water just like they had at Fort Bragg.

John heard someone open the front door. He stood to the side of the door to the kitchen where his dad wouldn't see him when he came to the kitchen. He wanted to surprise him.

His Dad walked to the table, set his lunch box down, and spoke to his wife. "Pretty hard day today. What's for supper?" he asked. "I'm really hungry."

John slipped up behind his Dad, put his hand on his shoulder and said, "Hi, Dad.".

When John's father turned around and saw John, he was speechless. He just put his arms around John and said, "Welcome home son. Good to see that you made it through that awful war. We all missed you very much."

The girls were the next ones home, and when they saw their big brother they were both hugging him and screaming,

"John! John! You're back home!"

When Joe, Johns brother, the last one of John's family to arrive home, saw his big brother, he shook his hand and gave him a little hug. It was nothing like he got from the others.

"Better get washed-up and ready for supper," John's mother said. "When we finish eating and get the dishes put away, we will all go to the living room and John can tell us all about where he went and about the War.

All the work in the kitchen was finished and the family were all together, the first time in over three years. Seems like old times when we lived on Little Sam," John's mom said. "I want to tell John what we have done since he went off to the War. Then he can tell us about what he has done."

She began, "Not long after you were home the last time, your dad said that he was going to find work in town and we would move off the mountain. He said the girls needed to go to a proper school and that the it was getting harder for him to make a living on the mountain. The first place he asked about a job was at the paper mill. He was lucky. They were hiring a few workers, and he got a job. The pay is good: twenty dollars a week, and if he works extra sometimes he gets twenty-five dollars.

"We loaded all our belongings on the sled, hooked the horse to it, and left our house on the mountain. Dad had a man with a wagon to haul our things to town from the gap in the mountain on Crabtree Road. We didn't have much to move. All the furniture you see here we bought after moving.

"The girls started to the school not far from here. It's called North Canton School. They finished there and are now at the Canton High School. One will finish this year, and the other next year.

"Joe, your brother is working with a contractor who builds houses and other buildings. He is learning the electrical trade.

"Now it's your turn," John's mother said.

"Well, you know about a few places I went to," John said. "I told you about them in the letters I wrote you. I never wrote you about getting shot and having to go to the hospital. I didn't want to worry you about it. I am as good as new now. The Army has the best doctors in the world."

John and his family talked until it was getting late when John said, "We better get to bed and get some rest. Dad has to go to work, the girls have to go to school, and Joe to work. I want to get up early, also. I'm thinking of walking up Little Sam and seeing the old home place once more.

They said good night and all went off to bed.

Sarah

John was up and in the kitchen with his mother before the rest of the family were ready for breakfast.

"Mom, have you seen or heard anything about the Smiths"?

"Haven't seen or heard anything about them since we moved to town," she said. "May still be on Little Sam. Guess the reason you ask is you are interested in seeing Sarah, their daughter."

John didn't answer or continue the conversation. "Is breakfast about ready?" he asked his mom. "I'm as hungry as a bear."

"About ready to put the food on the table," his mom said. The biscuits are nearly done."

When all the family were seated at the table and John's dad had asked the blessing, it was everyone for himself. There was very little talking. Everyone except John and his mother had to eat and get off to work or school.

"Guess I had better get started up Little Sam if I expect to get back before dark," John said.

"I'll fix you a couple of biscuits with the ham that was left from breakfast," his mother said. "You may get hungry before supper time."

"After I go to our house, I may drop by the Smiths'. I could eat dinner with them."

"Better take the biscuits, just in case," his mom said.

John took the biscuits and left.

It was about noon time when John arrived at the old house where he was born and grew up. The door was open, and he could see that there had been animals inside. Before he left, he found a piece of wire and tied the door shut.

"Sarah and me may have to live here until we get our house built on the next ridge," John said.

John headed toward where the Smiths lived. The trail was grown up with weeds and small bushes. It looked like it hadn't been used since he left over three years ago.

He was soon across the ridge and could see the Smith place. He squinted his eyes to see if he could see anyone. He didn't see anyone, and there wasn't any smoke from the chimney. When he got to the house, he could see that there was no one living there. He was very disappointed.

"I'll go down the hollow to where Granny Anderson lives. She has lived in that old log house all of her life. She never married and has delivered most all the babies on this mountain. I've heard Mom talk about her. Said that she was the best midwife in the whole county. And she was known to know all the news for miles around."

Granny Anderson's house was not too far from the Crabtree Road that went back to Canton. Granny was sitting in her rocking chair on the porch of her cabin when John got there.

"Howdy, Miss Anderson," John said. "Don't think you recognize me. I am the oldest boy in the Dowdy family who lived on the next ridge over," John said.

"You sure have grown since I brought you into this world. Been about twenty years ago, I guess," she said. "How is the family?"

"Fine," John said. "They moved to town while I was gone to the War. Do you know anything about the Smith family?" John asked. "I came by their house, but no one lives there anymore."

"The Smith family moved to town about two years ago. Haven't heard hide nor hair from them since they left."

"Thank you for telling me about the Smiths," John said. "I better get back to Canton. Don't want to get caught in the dark in these mountains. Good bye, Miss Anderson."

When John got to the city limits the sun had already gone down, and the streetlights were on. It wouldn't be any trouble finding the house on North Main.

When he arrived at his home the family had already eaten supper and were in the living room. The girls were getting their school work done. John's dad, mom and brother Joe were listening to the radio.

His mom asked, "Have you eaten supper yet?"

"No," John said. "Got anything left from supper?"

"Not a thing, but I'll fix you something," she said.

"No need for you to do that," John said. "I'll go down to the Greek café and get a couple of hotdogs. Sort of craving one. You want to come along with me?" he said to his brother Joe.

"I'd better not," Joe said. "I'm pretty tired. Had a rough day."

"We want to go. We want to go," the girls said.

"Come on," John said to his little sisters. "We can't stay long. You have to finish your homework."

John left the house with his sisters hanging onto his arms, one on each side.

They were sitting on the stools at the café eating their hotdogs when the older girl said to John, I saw that Smith girl the other day. I was in the dime store. I think she works there. She spoke to me, but I don't think she knew me.

"I wish you had asked her where she lived," John said. "Hurry and finish eating. We got to get back to that homework."

The next morning John was awake when everyone was getting ready to go to work and school. He didn't get out of bed until everyone was gone but his mom. He dressed and went to the kitchen where his breakfast was on the table.

His mom sat down at the table with John and asked, "What are you going to do today? Wouldn't mind if you stayed around. We could do some catching-up on what you did during the War," his mom said.

"Guess I'll try to find where the Smiths live. I would like to find out what Sam has been doing since I've been gone."

John didn't see her, but his Mom was smiling. She knew who John wanted to see: Sarah, Sam.

"I'll go to the Post Office and ask them about the Smiths, John said. "They know where everyone lives in the town of Canton. I'll try to be back before Dad gets home from work.".

He went to the bathroom and looked in the mirror to make sure his cap was straight on his head. He wanted to look his best just in case he found the Smiths and Sarah.

He entered the Post Office and waited until there was no one else there except the postal clerk.

"Can I help you?" the clerk asked John.

"I hope you can," John said. "I have been gone from here for over three years. There is a family who I knew before I left that I would like to see. The trouble, though, is that they moved, and I don't know where to."

"What's their name?"

"Smith. I don't know what the man's first name is. We always called him 'Mister Smith'. He has a son named Sam and a daughter called Sarah. That is all I know about them.

"Smith ... Sarah Smith. I recall a Sarah Smith who came here several times to pick up mail about two years ago. The last time she was in she said they had moved to town and to send her mail to their house."

The postman went to a filing cabinet and began looking at cards in one of the drawers.

"Smith ... Smith ... Sarah Smith ... Ah ha! Here we are. I know exactly where they live," he said to John.

He closed the drawer and turned to face John. Do you know where the corn mill is on Beaverdam Creek?" he asked John.

"Sure do," John said. "Uncle Tom runs the mill. I know exactly where it is."

The clerk continued, "Before you get to the mill, there is an iron bridge that crosses the river. This is where lots of houses are. They were built for the workers at the paper mill. They call this Fiberville. Cross the bridge and go to the top of the hill. After you pass all the houses in Fiberville you are going into a village called Phillipsville. A wooded section starts at the top of the hill. There are two houses on the right and one on the left. The Smiths live in the first one on the right. Think you can find it?" the postman asked John.

"I think I can. Thank you for taking the time to help me find them," John said.

"No trouble at all. Glad to help. You sure look sharp in that Army uniform," the clerk said.

John left the Post Office and went on his way to the Smith's house and Sarah.

John crossed the bridge, and as he climbed the crooked road with houses on both sides, his head was spinning from all the things that he would say to Sarah when he met her after being away for three years.

When John was at the top of the hill in Fiberville, he saw the houses that the postman described to him. He slowed his pace and was soon on the porch of the Smith's home. He knocked on the door and waited. Soon the door opened.

"John Dowdy!" Mrs. Smith hollered. "When did you get home? My, you have grown and are about the most handsome young man I ever seen. Come on in," she said.

"Glad I found where you live," John said. "I went to where you used to live on the mountain. After I saw that you and your family were gone, I went to Granny Anderson's house and asked where had you moved to. She didn't know exactly but said you probably moved to town. The postman at the Post Office told me how to get here."

"We moved off the mountain about two years ago. Sam and his dad both got a job in the paper mill. All the children are in school except Sarah. She lives next door.

"Why is Sarah not living with you?" "John asked.

"Guess you had better go and ask her," Mrs. Smith said.

She looked down at the floor and said, "Go on, John, and surprise her."

John left Mrs. Smith standing at the door as went next door. He knocked on the door, and when Sarah opened it and saw John, she didn't say anything. Neither did John. They stood staring at each other.

John couldn't believe this was Sarah standing before him. Instead of the pretty young girl he remembered, standing before him was a girl with unkempt hair wearing a wrinkled house coat that was way too large, and she looked tired.

Sarah finally said, "John, I wasn't expecting you. Won't you come in. I need to tell you something."

"Hi, Sarah," John said as he followed Sarah into the living room.

After they were seated, Sarah hung her head and said, "John, I didn't wait for you. I am married and will have a baby in another four months."

"Why didn't you wait for me?" John asked.

"Let me tell you how it all happened," Sarah said. When we moved off the mountain, I was too old to go to school, so I got a job in the dime store. Bob, the son of the owner of the store, was the manager. He began to ask me to go to the café with him for lunch. Then we went to the moving picture show nearly every Saturday night. One night after the movie he walked me home. I started into the house when he said, 'Sarah, will you marry me?'

"'I'll have to think about it,' I said. 'I'll let you know Monday.'

"I began to think, 'I am nearly eighteen years old. What if John don't come back?' I asked myself a million things and then decided to marry Bob. 'If I don't get married soon I will be too old and no one will have me.' So on Monday, I told Bob I would marry him.

"He is a good to me and treats me real good. His Dad bought this house for us as a wedding present. "I'm sorry, John," Sarah said. "I dreamed about you every night and about the house we were going to build after we were married. I wish I had waited a few more months."

John saw that there were tears running down Sarah's cheeks. He stood up and started toward the door. "I wish you and your husband a long and happy marriage," John said as he left Sarah standing in the room.

Sarah said to John, "If it's a boy, I'll name him 'John.'"

It was a long, slow, and sad walk back to the house on North Main for John.

When he went into the house, his mom and all the others in the family saw that something was wrong. John was not the happy person that was there that morning. They didn't ask him any questions.

John didn't sleep too well that night. He was asking himself what he should do now that all his dreams were shattered. "I'll think of something," John told himself.

John didn't go anywhere after his visit to the Smiths. He spent most of his time talking to his mom. He told her about the girl, Pam, he meet at the fish and chips shop in England.

"I may go back to England someday and visit the café where Pam worked," John said to his mom. Pam said that she would like to see America someday. Or I may re-enlist in the Army. Been thinking about it a lot for the last few days.

This was not the end of the world for John Dowdy, but it was the end of his many dreams of marrying Sarah Smith and living on Little Sam Mountain.

The author, Charles C Fletcher has published two other books
Out West and Back and
The Panther on Cold Mountain and Other Stories.

The stories in Charles Fletcher's books are from his memories of his growing
up in the mountains of Western North Carolina.